Best Time

白 马 时 光

The Peculiar Life of a Lonely Postman Lonely Postman Lonely Postman Lonely
e Peculiar Life of a Lonely Postman Lonely Postman Lonely Postman Lonely
e Peculiar Life of a Lonely Postman Lonely Postman Lonely
The Peculiar Life of a Lonely Postman Lonely Postman Lonely
The Peculiar Life of a Lonely Postman Lonely Postman Lonely

The Peculiar Life of a Lonely Postman Lonely Postman Lonely

The Peculiar Life of a Lonely Postman Lonely Postman Lonely
he Peculiar Life of a Lonely Postman Lonely Postman Lonely The Peculiar Life

孤独邮差

〔加拿大〕丹尼斯·特里奥特 著 / 刘勇军 译

百花洲文艺出版社
BAIHUAZHOU LITERATURE AND ART PRESS

图书在版编目（CIP）数据

孤独邮差 /（加）丹尼斯·特里奥特著 ; 刘勇军译
. — 南昌：百花洲文艺出版社，2018.8
ISBN 978-7-5500-2852-4

Ⅰ.①孤… Ⅱ.①丹… ②刘… Ⅲ.①长篇小说—加
拿大—现代 Ⅳ.① I711.45

中国版本图书馆 CIP 数据核字（2018）第 107870 号

江西省版权局著作权合同登记号：14-2018-0074

THE PECULIAR LIFE OF A LONELY POSTMAN (THE POSTMAN'S ROUND) By
DENIS THERIAULT
Copyright © 2005, XYZ
This edition was licensed by Allied Authors Agency Through BIG APPLE AGENCY, INC.,
LABUAN, MALAYSIA.
Simplified Chinese edition copyright © 2018 by Beijing White Horse Time Culture
Development Co., Ltd.
All rights reserved.

孤独邮差 GUDU YOUCHAI

〔加拿大〕丹尼斯·特里奥特　著　　　刘勇军　译

出 版 人	姚雪雪
出 品 人	李国靖
特约监制	王 瑜
责任编辑	袁 蓉
特约策划	王 瑜
特约编辑	王 婷 李 肖
封面设计	小 贾
版式设计	王雨晨 赵梦菲
版权支持	韩东芳 李若昕
出版发行	百花洲文艺出版社
社 址	南昌市红谷滩世贸路 898 号博能中心 Ⅰ 期 A 座 20 楼 邮编 330038
经 销	全国新华书店
印 刷	北京中科印刷有限公司
开 本	880mm×1230mm 1/32
印 张	8.5
字 数	140 千字
版 次	2018 年 8 月第 1 版第 1 次印刷
书 号	ISBN 978-7-5500-2852-4
定 价	42.00 元

赣版权登字：05-2018-228
版权所有，侵权必究
发行电话 0791-86895108　　　　　网 址 http://www.bhzwy.com
图书若有印装错误，影响阅读，可向承印厂联系调换。

献给

露易丝和盖伊

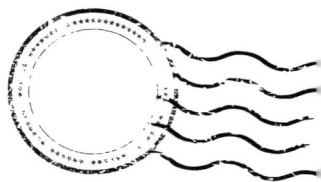

第一章

时光若流水，

彷徨复彷徨，

恋恋崎岖礁石上。

　　虽然此街名为山毛榉大街，道路两旁却多是些枫树。一眼望去，可以看到两排四五层楼高的公寓楼，屋外的楼梯可以直达顶层。街上一共有 115 个这样的楼梯，加起来共有 1495 级台阶。比洛多之所以门儿清，是因为他隔三岔五地便会数一次，也因为他每天早上都会爬楼梯。一共 1495 级台阶，每级台阶的高度约为 20 厘米，这样加起来就是 299 米，高度是玛利亚城的1.5 倍。真要算起来，比洛多每天在这些台阶上走的路相当于爬一遍埃菲尔铁塔了。

　　他每天风雨无阻，更别说忙活完后他还得回到城里。虽然比洛多每天不辞辛劳地爬上爬下，却并没有觉得有多了不起，顶多算是每天的一项挑战。要是没有这个挑战，他的生活怕是索然无味。他把自己当成了运动员，跟那种长距离远足的人差不多。不过，他总是莫名觉得遗憾，一想起这事就感到惋惜，在那些令人艳羡的耐力体育项目中，可没有爬楼梯比赛。要是有上下 1500 级台阶，或是上下 250 米的比赛，他准是个高手。要是奥运会有爬楼梯这个项目，比洛多一准儿能获得参赛资格，说不定还能拿块金牌，风风光光地站在最高领奖台上。

不过眼下他只是一名邮差。

一名 27 岁的邮差。

比洛多在圣·让维耶·埃姆这片儿做邮差已经五年了。为了方便工作，他甚至还搬到了这个以工薪阶层为主的地区生活，就住在街区的中心地带。他一直兢兢业业地工作着，这么多年来，要不是因为父母在魁北克坐缆车出了意外，他请了一天假参加父母的葬礼，比洛多就从来没有旷过一天工，绝对算得上一名忠心耿耿的员工。

早上，他会在分理处把每天要投递的邮件拣出来，把所有待送的信件和包裹分类整理，打好包。邮递员会用一辆小货车把邮件挨家挨户地送到邮筒里。尽管这项工作特别单调，但比洛多效率奇高。他在分拣邮件时自有一套方法，要说这个法子还是从赌场的发牌员和飞刀高手那里学来的。他手一甩，信就会如同飞刀一样不偏不倚地命中目标，落入相应的分拣箱中，很少失手。这个本事让他能比其他人早点儿收工，这当然是好事，因为他可以提前下班。早上，他一个人漫步街头，呼吸着新鲜、芬芳的空气，谁也不会对他指手画脚，怕是没有比这更惬意的生活了。

　　不过，生活也不总是顺风顺水。他还得分发那些皱巴拉唧的小广告，有时也会腰痛病犯了，扭伤了，还会碰到一些司空见惯的小灾小祸。夏天，酷暑令人窒息；秋天，倾盆大雨把人淋个透心凉；冬天，整座城市会变得天寒地冻，冷得彻骨，说不定有什么危险正等着他，这种日子都是邮差的天敌。不过，虽然总有不如意的时候，但一想到整个社区还真缺不了他，比洛多每每都会感到莫大的满足感，他觉得，虽说自己干的只是些微不足道的小事，却发挥着不可或缺的作用，他已经跟社区融为了一体。在他看来，投递信件是他必须兢兢业业完成的使命，他在以自己的方式为维持世界的运转做出贡献，这点他早就认准了。谁也甭想跟他换工作，除非对方也是邮差。

　　比洛多通常在玛德琳诺餐厅吃午饭，那家餐厅离分理处不远，吃过甜点后，他会花点时间练字，书法艺术可是个精细活儿，而他只是个半吊子。比洛多拿出练习本和钢笔，坐在吧台前，从报纸或者菜单上找几个字，开始写起来。他沉浸于那些字跃然纸上的感觉，笔往下一拉，往上一挑，用意大利字体书写的字好似在跳华尔兹，用饱满的安色尔字体书写的字则像是在表演沃尔特舞，而用哥特体写的字则犹如两柄交锋的利剑。他想象自己是中世纪受人尊敬的抄写僧侣，那些人终日跟笔墨相伴，虽然有损眼睛，手指也会冻得僵硬，但他们的灵魂却熠熠生辉。

比洛多在分理处的同事很是不解。他们吵吵闹闹，蜂拥进入玛德琳诺餐厅吃饭的时候，瞧见比洛多在练字免不了嘲笑一番，说他的那些字是鬼画符。比洛多倒也不生气，因为这些人是他的朋友，要说他们应该为自己的无知感到无地自容才对。除非像他这种见多识广，对书法持之以恒的人，谁又能领略得了一笔一画的美妙，欣赏得了这种干净利落的文字？他唯一的知音似乎是女招待塔尼娅。她总是一副和蔼可亲的样子，对他的字表现出了浓厚的兴趣，夸赞他写得很漂亮。还别说，这个年轻的女子真是个识趣的人，比洛多很喜欢她，每回都给她不少小费。要是他稍微细心一点，还会发现她经常从收银台附近瞄他。但他并没有发现，或许是他故意的也说不准。

自从塞格琳进入他的生活，他的眼里便没有了别的女人。

比洛多住在一幢高层住宅的十楼，跟他的金鱼比尔一起共享这个粘满了电影海报的单居室公寓。晚上，他会玩《光环》或者《使命召唤》游戏，然后边吃快餐边看电视。他几乎很少外出，除非罗伯特一再邀请，他偶尔才会在周五出去。罗伯特是他在邮局的同事，也是他最好的朋友，负责收集邮筒里的信件。罗伯特经常外出，几乎每晚都会出去。但就算朋友生拉硬拽，比洛多一般也不会答应，他不是很喜欢乌烟瘴气的夜总会、震耳欲聋的聚会场所和脱衣舞俱乐部。他宁愿待在家中，远离喧嚣的世界，远离那些搔首弄姿的女人。

自从塞格琳进入他的生活后，他更是如此。

总之，他晚上有更好的消遣，待在自己的公寓里忙得不亦乐乎。看完电视，洗完碗碟后，他会闩上门，一头扎进自己邪恶的小秘密中。

第二章

比洛多是个不怎么安分的邮差。他经手的邮件不计其数，多数没什么特别的，但是偶尔会碰上几封私人信件，在电子邮件盛行的当下，信越来越少，毕竟，物以稀为贵。每次发现私人信件的时候，比洛多都会异常兴奋，好比是在淘金盘中发现了一块金子。他不会立马把信送出去，而是带回家，用蒸汽把信封打开。晚上，他就一个人在房间里偷偷忙活这事。

比洛多是个好奇心很重的邮差。

他从来没收到过私人信件。他倒也想，但他并没有什么亲近到会给他寄信的朋友。以前他给自己寄过信，后来觉得还是没什么意思，慢慢也就罢手了。他并不怀念那些信，别人寄的信远比自己写的有吸引力，那才叫真正的信，是由现实中的人一笔一画写成的。然后，他表面上会波澜不惊地等着回信，其实内心却满心欢喜，相较于那些通过冰冷的键盘和用互联网即时进行沟通的人，选择写信这种方式是人们刻意为之，有人甚至会将其当成一种原则，一种生活方式，用不着分秒必争，自然也不会当成一种负担。

他看过桃乐丝·T从加斯佩半岛的玛利亚寄给妹妹格温多琳的信，讲述当地的一些奇闻逸事，读来十分有趣；他还读过被囚禁在卡捷港监狱的理查德·L写给小儿子雨果的叫人潸然泪下的信；还有里莫斯基圣·罗塞尔修道院的修女雷吉娜寄给老友杰曼的信，那些信洋洋洒洒，带有神秘的宗教主义色彩；还有远在育空省的年轻护士蕾蒂西娅为她的孤独未婚夫写的情色小故事；此外，还有位神秘的O先生寄出的信，向召唤神灵的N先生提供建议，古怪得很。这些信的内容五花八门，来自五湖四海。写信的人既有近在咫尺的亲人，也有相隔万里的朋友；既有啤酒品评师交流的心得，也有周游世界的人写给母亲的信；有退休的蒸汽火车锅炉工在信中历数身上大大小小的伤痕；有驻阿富汗的士兵写给心急如焚的妻子的信，言之凿凿，尽是些安慰妻子的话；还有忧心忡忡的舅舅写给外甥女的信，吩咐她们务必保守秘密；也有拉斯维加斯的杂技演员写给前男友或者前女友的绝交信，有的信中满腔愤懑，似乎隔着信封也能瞥见里面的内容。

但最多的还得算是情书了。就算情人节已经过了，爱情仍然是芸芸众生老生常谈的话题。这些爱情以不同形式的语法和语气糅合而成，以各种你想得到的方式跃然纸上。或是情意绵绵，或是彬彬有礼，或是脉脉传情，或是洁白无瑕，或是安之若素，或是慷慨激昂，偶尔还会如火山一样喷涌而出。多数情况下都是充满诗情画意的，尤其是那些以简单的语言表达的感情才会让人怦然心动，如若将感情隐藏在字里行间反而不会那么感动，因为在不痛不痒的字句中，爱情的火花已经慢慢消失得无影无踪了。

比洛多会反复阅读当天的信件，对信的内容早已如数家珍，然后他会把这些信件复印、存档，根据主题的不同，按颜色分类放在一个文件夹中，再将文件放在防火的档案柜中。最后，他会把信原封不动地塞回去，娴熟地封好，隔天再投入收件人的信箱中，像是什么也没发生过。这档子事情他已经在私下里偷偷干了两年。他很清楚自己是在犯罪，但在好奇心的驱使下，他的那点罪恶感早就被抛到九霄云外去了。反正又不会伤害到谁，只要他继续小心翼翼，也用不着冒多大的风险——谁又会担心信晚送了一天呢？再说了，从信寄出的那天算起，谁又知道信被耽搁了呢？

比洛多通过这种方式截留了三十来封信。要是把这些信的情节凑在一起，准能炮制出一部肥皂剧，起码也能凑成半部，因为信的另一半在别人手里，他看不到。但他喜欢想象另一半故事情节的发展，尽心尽力地写回信，虽然他从未将这些信发出去，但等他再次收到回信的时候，他每次都会惊讶地发现信的内容跟他那些从未寄出的信如此相似。

事情的经过就是这样，比洛多在体验别人的生活。相对于无聊的现实生活，他更喜欢信里这种如同连续剧一样的生活，更加丰富多彩，也更加刺激。在这个由私密的信件构成的虚幻世界中，让他欲罢不能的莫过于塞格琳的信了。

第三章

　　塞格琳住在瓜德罗普岛的皮特尔角，她会定期给一个叫加斯顿·格朗普雷的男子写信，此人租住在山毛榉大街的一套公寓里。算起来，比洛多截留她的信已经有两个年头了，每次分拣信件的时候，比洛多只要一看到塞格琳的信，就会莫名地生出一种敬畏之情，激动得浑身战栗。他会不露声色地把信塞进口袋里，只有当他一个人走在路上的时候，他激动的心情才会溢于言表，一遍一遍地把玩着信封，满怀期待地用手指体验那份兴奋。他本可以当场拆开，欣赏信里的文字，但他宁愿等待。所以，在他勇敢地把信塞进口袋前，他会闻一闻信封上散发的橘子香味儿，这种稍纵即逝的快乐让他陶醉其中，他整天都会把信揣在贴着心窝的口袋里，强忍着看信的冲动。他得把这份快乐留到晚上，等到洗完碗碟后，这一刻终于来临了。他会滴几滴柑橘油，点上几根蜡烛，在唱片机上放一盘心旷神怡的挪威爵士乐。最后，他会启开信封，将信轻轻地拿出来，欣赏里面的内容：

伶俐初生儿，

碧波清如许，

儿如水獭当中嬉。

　　读到这样的文字，比洛多有种身临其境的感觉，仿佛亲眼看到一个光着身子的小孩在碧波荡漾的婴儿游泳池朝他游过来，把他当成了妈妈。小孩像是正朝她的美人鱼妈妈游过去，妈妈张开双臂，瞪着一双犹如蝾螈一般的蓝色眼睛看着他。婴儿并不知道自己不会游泳，但他没有忘记自己的本能。他从没见过水，也不知道水是危险的，可能淹死他。婴儿全然没有理会这些，只管依靠自己的本能在水里划拉着，他紧紧地抿着嘴，在池中游泳。比洛多仿佛清楚地看到一只小小的鳍足类动物在波光粼粼的水下划过，那个小家伙活像一只有趣的小精灵，皮肤跟婴儿一样满是褶皱，鼻孔不停地冒着泡泡。比洛多不由得哈哈大笑，因为他不曾料到会是这样有趣又让人动容的画面。他想象着自己也漂浮在水中，仿佛听到了水流拍打耳膜发出的嗡嗡声，他感觉自己正跟那个婴儿在池中游泳。这就是塞格琳写的这首奇妙的小诗带来的暗示性力量，可以让他切切实实地感受，亲眼见到那些场景。

孤 独 邮 差

　　瓜德罗普岛的那个女人的信里只有一首小诗，再无其他，
一页纸上只有一首诗，内容不多，却丝毫不会让人觉得空洞，
因为那些诗也跟整部小说一样给读者充分的营养，在你的内心
深处，这样的诗堪称长篇大作，会永远在灵魂深处回荡。比洛
多对这些诗歌已经烂熟于心，早上还会自顾自地背诵。他将这
些信珍藏在床头柜最上面的抽屉里，晚上，他喜欢将这些信都
展开，连成一个神秘的圆形图案，将自己围在当中，反复阅读：

　　　　　　　　冰川不识途，
　　　　　　　碎云镶天际，
　　　　　　碧落流沙云飘扬。

　　　　　　　　蜘蛛蟹最终，
　　　　　　纵身一跃后，逃离，
　　　　　　　竖琴螺的壳。

　　　　　　　　街头乒唰响，
　　　　　　　窗户钉住了，
　　　　　　飓风欲来风满楼。

入夜，大海上，
鲨鱼吃着太阳鱼，
打起了哈欠。

微微夏日风，
轻轻撩起了台布，
碗儿齐跳舞。

　　塞格琳的诗虽然在内容和风格上迥然不同，但在形式上却很相似，因为所有诗都只有三句话，其中两行是五个音节，另一行是七个音节，加一起不多不少一共十七个音节。全是这种神秘的结构，像是遵循了某种规则。比洛多总觉得这不可能是巧合，他想了好几个月，脑袋都想破了。一天，他终于发现了其中的奥秘。

　　那是一个礼拜天的早上，他在玛德琳诺餐厅一边吃早餐，一边看娱乐版的副刊。突然，他看到报纸的最上面好像有三行短诗，一下儿被咖啡呛住了。这首诗的其中两行是五个音节，一行是七个音节，不过让他失望的是，这首诗只是讽刺当下的时事。但这个专栏的标题却让他眼前一亮："礼拜六俳句。"

　　比洛多匆忙跑回家，在字典里找到了这个词：

　　"俳句：1.一种日本短诗，一共三行，十七个音节，通常描写自然景物。2.其他语言模仿日本短诗做的诗。"

　　原来如此。

　　这就是瓜德罗普岛的那个女人写的诗。

　　自那时起，比洛多经常去图书馆翻阅各种有关俳句的诗——这些书都是从日语翻译过来的，因此他还认识了不少知名作者。比如松尾芭蕉、种田山头火、永田爱，还有小林一茶。但没有谁的诗能达到塞格琳的效果，因为那些诗不能把他带到遥远的地方，让他真真切切地去看，去感受她诗中描绘的意境。

　　而且塞格琳写得一手好字，更加让她的诗有了这种神奇的魔力，因为她在表达自己的情感时，用的是更为细腻、优雅的意大利体，比洛多觉得能欣赏到这样的文字真是三生有幸。塞格琳的字线条饱满，极富想象力，向下的一笔拉得很长，往上的一提饰以大量圆圈和精致的点，让她的字看起来落落大方，让人称奇的是，塞格琳写的每个字都以三十度的角度倾斜，看起来毫无瑕疵，字母之间的间距相当匀称。塞格琳的字真是让人赏心悦目，看到她的字好比是服用了一剂良药，听到了一曲天籁之音，说是一首书法盛宴的交响乐也不为过，堪称封神之作。她的字是如此美妙，让人感动得想哭。他曾在什么地方看过这样一句话：字如其人。

比洛多认准了塞格琳的心灵定是出尘不染。天使的字也莫过于此。

第四章

　　比洛多知道塞格琳是皮特尔角的一名小学老师，还知道她是个可人儿，因为比洛多曾见过她寄给格朗普雷的照片，八成是一封回复对方希望交换照片的信，照片背面还有一行字："很高兴通过照片认识您。现在附上本人照片一张，是我跟孩子们的合影。"照片中，她被一群笑容灿烂的孩子围在当中，但比洛多只关心她的笑容，眼里也只有那翠绿色的眼眸，如同海浪拍打峭壁发出的阵阵回声。他扫描并打印了那张照片，裱在相框里，放在床头柜上，而她的那些俳句就珍藏在床头柜的抽屉里。现在，他每天晚上睡觉前都会含情脉脉地看着塞格琳的照片，日有所思夜有所梦：她笑意盈盈、明眸善睐，五官极为出众。他还梦见同她在海滨浪漫地散步，玛丽－加兰特岛在薄暮中若隐若现，橙色的浮云掠过天空，风儿轻拂他们的头发，那些俳句也让他的梦境充满了奇思妙想。他会梦见跟她一起蹦极，两人一起下落，长长的绳子绷紧后，一头扎进芳香四溢的海中，他们在珊瑚礁中跟太阳鱼、小小的两栖动物一起游泳，鲨鱼茫然地在四周游来游去。

比洛多从未想过自己会无可救药地爱上一个人。塞格琳已经完全俘获了他的心，他不由得感到害怕——担心无法左右自己的生活。可那些俳句真的具有魔力，他哪里还顾得上担心，反而觉得无比幸福，他感谢幸运女神能够眷顾他，让他在人生的道路上能够遇到瓜德罗普岛这个漂亮的女人。不过，一想到塞格琳的信其实是写给另一个男人的，他就不由得心生嫉妒，开心不起来了。每次他看完塞格琳新写的诗，重新将信放进信封，第二天再将信投到他的情敌加斯顿·格朗普雷的邮箱时，他真是羡慕得要命。那家伙是怎样认识塞格琳的？他到底是她什么人？照片背后的话以及那些诗歌的意思倒是能证明他们只不过是普通的朋友关系，想到这个，比洛多会稍微感到慰藉。但是，那些信毕竟都是寄给格朗普雷的，这小子可真幸运，信才是重点。

　　比洛多偶尔会在门口瞥见这名男子。那人胡子拉碴，不修边幅，头发也乱蓬蓬的，总是穿着一件鲜红的便袍，看起来像是晚上压根儿就没睡过觉。他就像个疯疯癫癫的科学家，整天牢骚满腹。要说这人还真是个怪胎。比洛多心想，也不知道这家伙在门垫里发现塞格琳写给他的信后作何反应？他会迫不及待地拆开，徜徉在她的文字里吗？他也会跟自己一样觉得兴奋异常吗？塞格琳的信也会让他有身临其境的感觉吗？也会跟自己一样浮想联翩吗？他又会怎样回信呢？

下午，比洛多回家时会再次经过玛德琳诺餐厅，有时看到格朗普雷在里面，抿着咖啡，在笔记本上写着什么，看起来很是得意。在写诗吗？要是自己也能写诗，让他做什么都愿意，他要是有这样的本事，准会给塞格琳回信，就好比给那些他幻想的笔友写信，但他可没这样的本事，没办法跟她一样写出那种精妙的诗篇。比洛多是那种一提到"诗"这样的字眼就会望而生畏的人。这样一个普普通通的邮差怎能在一夜之间摇身一变成为诗人？你还能指望鸵鸟会弹班卓琴，蜗牛能骑自行车不成？他倒也尝试写过一两回，结果可想而知，自然是羞得无地自容，再也不敢动笔，因为他害怕有损诗的本意，从而间接玷污了塞格琳那些神圣的作品。格朗普雷有这种罕见的才能吗？他会写俳句吗？

格朗普雷总得知道自己有多幸运吧？他对塞格琳的感情有比洛多对她的四分之一，甚至十分之一吗？

比洛多一方面对塞格琳崇拜不已，另一方面，他还深深地爱上了塞格琳出生的地方，正是有了那种得天独厚的自然环境，才会有这样一个可人儿。比洛多会把书店里旅游类的书搜罗一空，没完没了地在电脑上搜寻跟瓜德罗普岛有关的信息，了解群岛的地理环境、当地的饮食、音乐传统、朗姆酒的制作方法、人文历史、捕鱼技巧、植被情况以及建筑风格。他贪婪地了解各种信息，虽然从未去过那里，但比洛多俨然成了"蝴蝶岛"的专家。当然啦，他大可以去那里旅游，亲眼去看看瓜德罗普岛，不过，他从未认真考虑过这个想法，因为他是个名副其实的宅男，外出的想法让他焦躁不安。他并不想亲自去瓜德罗普岛，只想将那里的一草一木如同画卷一样都印在脑海里，这样才会符合他的梦境。他会将这些梦境放在现实的环境中，这样才能凸显塞格琳的美，他充分发挥自己的想象力，塞格琳的音容笑貌在他脑海中格外清晰。

比洛多梦见她骑着自行车沿杜马诺尔林荫大道朝他驶来，两边是郁郁葱葱的棕榈树。比洛多还梦见她下午放学后，或是在港湾漫步，或是在圣昂图万市场购物。她走过大集市五颜六色的小摊，小摊上无花果、香蕉、甘薯、白薯、辣椒、菠萝、番荔枝、黄肉芋、杨桃应有尽有，还有各种香料、肉桂、科伦坡粉、藏红花、香子兰、月桂和咖喱，这些东西混杂在一起，撩拨着人的感官，旁边还有潘趣酒、糖浆、糖果、编织物、鲜花、

孤 独 邮 差

长尾小鹦鹉和扫帚，另外还有药水，各种叫人心旷神怡、旺运
招财、永葆爱情的美酒佳肴和包治百病的灵丹妙药。

　　比洛多每个晚上都会在梦中与她相会，那些场景宛若一部
部如梦似幻的电影。片中女主角自然是塞格琳，背景便是瓜德
罗普岛：蜿蜒的羊肠小道，甘蔗田。陡峭的小路从遍地兰花和
茂盛的蕨类植物当中穿过，云雾缭绕的群山上大大小小的瀑布
自绿油油的青苔上倾泻而下。还有高耸入云的苏弗里埃尔火山，
虽然处于休眠期，却无时无刻不让人提心吊胆。灯火通明的村
庄全是红铁皮屋顶，墓地里满是镶嵌着贝壳、黑白相间的坟墓。
狂欢节、音乐会、大鼓手、一袭红衣的"女魔头"，还有那身
穿各色艳丽服装，在博拉鼓的鼓点下放纵扭动腰肢的舞娘，开
怀畅饮朗姆酒的人们。

　　他会梦见瓜德罗普岛上红树林沼泽地和番石榴、大小不一
的岛屿、水面下游过的蝠鲼，斑驳陆离的珊瑚礁、胭脂鱼、石
斑鱼、飞鱼，戴着帽子的勒桑特斯渔民正在补网。巴斯特尔北
部经年被海水冲击、参差不齐的石灰石海岸线。然后画面中会
突然出现静得出奇的小海湾和金黄色的海滩，塞格琳会在跟她
眼睛颜色一样蓝绿色的海浪中游泳，尔后，她刚从海浪中现身，
优雅地回到海滩上时，阳光便迫不及待地照在她身上，似要赢

得女神的芳心。她赤裸着身子，漫步走过沙滩，胸脯上布满的水珠儿，慢慢在长着金黄色绒毛的小腹上蒸发了。

比洛多做着梦，并不奢求什么。他只想继续这样幻想，尽情享受这令他神魂颠倒的梦境，享受塞格琳的文字为他勾勒出的美妙景色。他唯一的愿望就是希望这个愉悦的梦永远都不会醒，他只想安安静静地享受这样的幸福时刻，谁也不要打扰他。可最终还是出事了。

第五章

　　那是八月的一个早上，大风肆虐，天上乌云密布，远处传来了轰隆隆的雷声，随时都会下雨，不过，比洛多一点儿也不担心，因为他相信邮局的雨衣非常防水，不管下多大的雨都奈何不了他。所以，不管老天爷想怎样使绊，都无法阻止他坚定的步伐。比洛多往返于山毛榉街，爬上一级又一级台阶，这时候，他碰到了朋友罗伯特，罗伯特刚把邮箱里的东西送到邮车里。

　　他们很少会在这样的场合下碰面，因为罗伯特拿到邮箱里的信后，比洛多往往已经离开了。不过，这次罗伯特解释说，他昨晚跟一个叫布兰达的美女疯狂了一整夜，睡过头了。两人互相打过招呼后，开起了善意的玩笑，比洛多想继续送信，不过罗伯特拦住了他，这小子有了一段新的艳遇，自然有说不完的话题，罗伯特建议今晚叫上布兰达和她的朋友——那可是个风骚女人——到时候他们可以成双成对地约会。听到这话，比洛多叹了一口气。罗伯特老是想介绍女友给他的这种行为实在令他厌烦。他的这位同事是实在看不惯比洛多这种单身的生活，认为这样的生活方式很不健康，还颇具讽刺意味地给他取了个

"力比多 ①"的绰号，自告奋勇地担任起了"红娘"的角色，恨不得让比洛多跟但凡能动弹的活物勾搭上，还瞒着比洛多在社交网站上为他注册了账号，将他的名字和电话登记在了流行杂志的求偶栏目上。

罗伯特的种种自作主张的行为让比洛多不胜其烦，害得他都不敢接电话了，他的语音信箱也常常被挤爆。但他并没有责怪罗伯特，因为他知道同事的出发点是好的。毕竟罗伯特弄出这么多事情，只是想帮他，但做过头了。罗伯特向来都是这样的人，不过，他还是比洛多在这个世界上最好的朋友，不是吗？比洛多也尝试去喜欢这个人，喜欢他的粗俗、自私、虚伪、投机取巧、撒谎成性的行为，甚至包括他的口臭。

尽管比洛多会原谅罗伯特在性格方面的小瑕疵，但他仍然不愿跟朋友一起到外面鬼混。可罗伯特这小子不是那种轻易打退堂鼓的人，所以比洛多必须找个说得过去的借口才行，还不能太蹩脚了，所以，眼看暴风雨即将来临，他还在绞尽脑汁地想法子。

这时，天空中突然响起了一声惊雷，像是一个巨大的薯片

① 性力。由弗洛伊德提出，泛指一切身体感官的快感。——编者注

孤 独 邮 差

袋在头顶炸开了，天空顿时出现了一道裂缝。大雨倾盆而下，能见度也就几米，罗伯特连忙把邮包扔进车里，邀请比洛多也赶紧上车，免得被淋成个落汤鸡。比洛多同意了，心想等到暴风雨停了再说，于是，他接受了邀请，绕到邮车的另一边。就在这时，马路对面有人大声喊了一句，吸引了他的注意力。比洛多转身一看，发现正是塞格琳的笔友格朗普雷，那家伙一年四季都穿着同样的便袍，正站在对面三楼的楼梯平台上。

格朗普雷打开雨伞，匆匆下了楼梯，使劲儿挥舞着手中的信，他显然是想赶在罗伯特开车离开前把信寄走。比洛多见他什么也不管，走到已经水流成河的马路上。他根本不在意路上有没有水，只管朝他们跑过来，大声呼喊着，叫他们等等，他根本没看到一辆卡车正从瓢泼大雨中朝他驶过来。比洛多伸出胳膊，大声喊着提醒格朗普雷小心，而卡车司机也将喇叭按得很响，可一切都太晚了。刹车发出尖锐的声音，轮胎划过满是雨水的路面，只听"砰"的一声，卡车似乎戛然停了下来，但出于惯性，车子仍然撞上了格朗普雷，他像一只巨大的布娃娃飞向了空中，跟着又重重地掉了下来，软绵绵地趴在离人行道十米远的地方。

所有的车都停了下来，世界也像是静止了。有那么一瞬间，周围只听到发动机空转的声音，雨水啪嗒啪嗒地砸在沥青路面上，车顶上的声响犹如擂鼓一般。已经完全看不清格朗普雷原来的样子了，要不是还在不时可怕地抽搐几下，怕是会被当成一堆从某人的胳膊下滑落的换洗衣服。罗伯特第一个反应过来，飞快跑了过去，比洛多跟在他后头，他们蹲在格朗普雷旁边，这会儿，那人软嗒嗒地躺在地上，伤得不轻，他的四肢以怪异的角度弯曲着，乱蓬蓬的胡子上沾满了血，虽然下着大雨，仍然没能把血冲干净。那个可怜的家伙还有意识，他用惊恐且难以置信的表情看着罗伯特，眼睫毛如同蝴蝶的翅膀一样不停扇动着，视线也因大雨变得模糊。他的右手仍然紧紧地攥着那封急待送出去的信，比洛多看到收信人正是塞格琳。

被鲜血染红的雨水朝下水道流去，格朗普雷看来是不行了。他拼命地呼吸着，比洛多看得出来，他快死了，但就在这时，格朗普雷发出奇怪的喘息声。比洛多惊得目瞪口呆，发现这个奄奄一息的人居然在笑。他没有看错，那人的声音刺耳、空洞，不带一点感情色彩，听着非常瘆人。比洛多不由得颤抖起来，然后发现身体哆嗦的人还不止他一个。其他的目击者也被这个将死之人喉咙里发出的恐怖笑声吓得不知所措。格朗普雷继续笑了一阵儿，像是把这事当成了一个痛心疾首的玩笑，他终于不再笑了，突然咳嗽起来，喷出了一团猩红的血。

　　格朗普雷费了好大的劲儿才别过头去，盯着手中那封被鲜血染红的信，这个时候，他仍然紧紧地把信攥在手里。格朗普雷闭上眼睛，牙关紧闭，他紧紧地抓着那封信，也不知道哪儿来的力气，像是为了证明他最后的那点儿意志。这时，他突然说话了，声音很小，比洛多和罗伯特只得俯身贴在他身上，才能听得见。他嘴里含糊不清地嘀咕着什么，好像是在说什么"换鞋"。说完后，突然一切都结束了。他的眼睑突然睁开，瞳孔放大，目光瞬时变得呆滞了。格朗普雷的眼睛里满是雨水，活像两洼小小的池塘。他临死前的那两个字像谜团一样，让比洛多百思不得其解，到底什么意思呢？有那么一瞬间，比洛多甚至忍不住看了看格朗普雷脚上的鞋，想看看是不是藏有什么东西。但他转念一想，兴许是他听错了，因为格朗普雷在临终前还在痛苦地呻吟，应该就是"回答"的意思。这个词难道不是暗示这个即将咽气的人正往未知的世界纵身一跃，已经准备好进入神秘的来世了？

　　就在这时，比洛多发现那封信已经不在死人的手里了，准是格朗普雷咽气的时候把手松开了，信也随着湍急的水流进入了下水道。可比洛多突然又在那群目瞪口呆的旁观者脚下看到了那封信，雨水凄凉地打着旋涡，那封信正远离旋涡的方向，往下水道格栅形成的"小瀑布"那边漂流。比洛多像是突然被电击中了，朝那封信冲了过去，他将围观的人群推向车祸发生的地点，他明白自己要不惜一切代价把信拿回来。比洛多跑过去，弯下身子，伸手去够那封信。他感觉自己的胳膊越来越长，拼命伸长手指……想要去抓住那封信……可就是差了那么一点点。信被下水道吞噬了，比洛多也因为惯性一个趔趄摔了个四脚朝天，躺在冰冷的水里。这时，一道闪电划过天际，那一瞬间，比洛多的心骤然凉了，那封信消失在了地下深处，他跟塞格琳联络的机会也消失了。

第六章

第二天，比洛多出门的时候，心情甭提有多沮丧了，他似乎觉得太阳也在为他惋惜，就像是它发出的只是过去黑白电影里那种冰冷的光。他来到山毛榉大街，在人行道上停了下来，也就是格朗普雷出事的地方，那里已经找不到昨天惨祸发生的一点点痕迹，水洼里甚至都找不到任何血迹，他不由得感到一丝悲凉。雨水把所有的一切都冲刷得干干净净。

那封信被下水道吞噬的场景不停在他脑海里闪过，久久无法忘怀。自己也太不小心了，一想到这个，他的心情格外难过。要是他能拿到那封信，看到信中的内容该多好啊，他至少知道格朗普雷在给塞格琳的信中写了什么。看过信后他还会把它寄出去吗？他在问自己。如果车祸可以避免，他八成会这么做。但现在想这个问题已经没有任何意义了。塞格琳不会收到那封信，所以也没回信的必要了，而比洛多怕是再也读不到她的诗了。格朗普雷的死结束了一切的美好，让他们再也没办法通信了，也让比洛多的生活少了一大乐趣。还有比这更无助的事吗？

过了一会儿，比洛多往这条大街相反的方向走去，来到死者的门口，将往常的账单和广告单塞进信箱里。他明知道这么做没有意义，到时候邮箱里的邮件会被堆得满满当当，最后，邮局会收到一封"要求终止投递服务"的信函。

他想象着这幢陌生公寓的内部构造，心情无比郁闷，此时此刻，周围一片沉寂，时间也仿佛停滞了，格朗普雷唯一留在人世的痕迹不过是几件家具，几样物品，几件一动不动挂在衣架上的衣服，几张照片和几本写写画画的本子。

格朗普雷的死并没有在街区引起多大的轰动，因为邻居对这个人几乎一无所知。而在玛德琳诺餐厅，塔尼娅在他经常喝咖啡的桌子上摆放了一枝康乃馨。仅此而已。看来我们离开这个世界的方式大抵如此，比洛多心想。或许不经意间就走了，一切都是那样的波澜不惊，甚至都不会留下一丝痕迹，如同燕子在天空中一闪而过，一只松鼠冒冒失失地跑到马路上，很快便会被人遗忘。

大概也就这样吧。

比洛多的生活似乎没有一点儿变化，他一大早就会起床，去上班，在玛德琳诺餐厅吃中饭，然后回家。他像往常一样平平淡淡地生活，但这一切都是表象，他的日常生活看上去风平浪静，却蕴含着连他本人都没有察觉到的细微变化。

起初，比洛多只是觉得疲惫，他将这种郁闷的心情归咎于季节的变化，认定只是白天越来越短，秋天即将来临引起的。但是，不久之后，他越发觉得心神不宁。一天晚上，比洛多像过去一样，偷看别人的信件，却意识到以前让他兴奋异常的事情突然变得索然无味。他最喜欢的肥皂剧也了无新意，没有什么有趣的情节能提起他的兴趣，别人生活中无论发生什么戏剧性的事情也都不再吸引他。

第二天，他在分理处工作时，再也没办法像平常那样轻轻松松地分拣邮件了。他往架子上扔信时，几乎每两次都会出一次错，所以，他只得按照传统的方法分拣信件。他上班时候也比平常晚了二十分钟，希望早晨清新的空气能让自己振奋起来，但痛苦地走了三公里后，他感觉一点儿劲都没有了。这还不算，后来在山毛榉大街挑战自己爬楼梯的时候，结果只走了短短24级台阶，便只得停下来大口喘气，最后，他完全咬紧牙关，休息了不下六次后才终于爬上最后一级台阶。他这是怎么啦？莫非是患了流感，身体吃不消了？

他来到玛德琳诺餐厅时，发现一点儿胃口都没有，平日里，他三下五除二就会把东西吃得光光，可现在他就点一份蔬菜汤，可就是这碗汤他都没喝完。他连写字的工具都懒得拿出来，他压根儿就没心情，不过，他还是按照平日的习惯做了，算是打发时间吧。他的脑子一片混乱，精神状况极不正常。他整个人都处于恍惚的状态中，脑子里不知在想些什么。他走到一个交叉路口的时候碰上了红灯，差点儿被一辆汽车撞倒。正所谓祸不单行，没过多久，比洛多在往一家人投递广告单的时候，被一只拴着狗链的狗给咬了，那家伙就只剩下一只眼睛，狗屋上面还写明了它叫"独眼巨人波吕斐摩斯"，那只畜生在他的右小腿上狠狠地咬了一口，还冲他一阵狂吠，这才引起狗主人的注意。最后，还是狗主人给了它一铁锹，那家伙才松口。看来人在倒霉的时候，放个屁都会砸脚后跟。

被狗咬了后，比洛多还得处理后续的麻烦事，他在急诊室足足等了六个小时，才打上狂犬疫苗，包扎好伤口，等到这段糟心的事结束后，天已经很晚了。在坐出租车回家的路上，比洛多真想挥舞着铁锹好好发泄一番，腿上剧烈的疼痛让他的火气越来越大。他很想反抗，但他一整天碰上的都是糟心事，难道诅咒阴魂不散地缠上了他？

孤 独 邮 差

　　一回到家，他便把自己锁在屋里，一瘸一拐地在起居室里走来走去，想找到发泄的出口。他打开电脑，把一腔怒气全撒在了西昂星球邪恶的叛乱分子上，疯狂杀戮那些长着触角的怪物，最后他不仅冲关成功，还创造了新的得分纪录，但他仍然难以平息心中翻肠搅肚的怒气。

　　等到最后去睡觉的时候，比洛多实在是累坏了，直到凝视着塞格琳的照片时，他的心绪才稍微平静下来。他想象着那个瓜德罗普岛漂亮的女人每天早上打开邮箱，满以为会收到格朗普雷的回信，可那封信却永远不会来了。比洛多倒也生出过这样的念头，写信告诉人家，她的笔友已经死了，但他不能这么做，因为真要写的话，不就把自己出卖了？等于不打自招，承认偷看了别人的信。也不知道塞格琳要等多久才会死心。

　　车祸发生后，山毛榉大街雷雨交加，但这次受害者不是格朗普雷，而是塞格琳，她躺在湿漉漉的沥青马路上，浑身是血，奄奄一息，是那样的无助。那个年轻的女人颤抖地朝比洛多伸出手，请求他不要忘记她……比洛多陡然惊醒，大口大口喘着气，一种寒冷刺骨的感觉向他袭来。他分不清到底是梦境还是现实，因为他被噩梦缠绕，恐怖的画面在他脑海里挥之不去。

比洛多一心只想摆脱紧紧攥住他的恐惧，于是，比洛多让塞格琳的俳句环绕着自己，以抵御黑暗的侵袭。他大声把那些诗句读了起来，像是在念护身符咒，可事与愿违，那些诗让他更加痛苦了，没有产生他预期的效果。因为那些诗刚从他嘴里说出，黑暗便把它们吞噬了，本该产生的让人慰藉的效果并没有出现。那些精心写就的俳句像是突然变得毫无意义，如同标本中枯萎的花，变得了无生趣，仅残存着一丝淡淡的气味。

比洛多抖动着那些诗篇，希望能够再次出现奇迹，结果只是把纸张弄得皱巴巴。就连塞格琳写的东西也让他提不起劲儿，那一瞬间，他生平第一次——绝对是头一次——觉得那般孤独。如同一个巨大的海浪将他吞没了，让他体会到了内心最深处的孤独，将他卷入深海的无尽黑暗中，在那里，强大的旋涡又将他卷入了一个长着血盆大口的深渊中，如同一个巨大的下水道口。他挥舞着手臂，想要找到什么攀附的东西，结果却只能触及他灵魂深处的孤独，让他痛苦不堪。

这时，比洛多莫名地清醒过来，他突然意识到自己的生命中不能没有塞格琳，没有她，他根本活不下去；没有她，他的生活将毫无意义。生活中的美、欲望、内心的宁静这些类似的抽象感情统统跟他无关，全都飘荡到了远方，他再也感觉不到了。他自己只不过是一块残骸，一艘没人掌舵、也没有动力的幽灵船，只会顺着洋流漂向远方，最后被马尾藻黏黏的网缠住，不再动弹，海藻缠住他的躯壳，把他拉到水里，沉入海底。

这是一幕多么恐怖的场景啊。故事难道只会这样愚蠢地结束吗？比洛多难道不应该做点什么，想想办法，避免悲剧的发生吗？他能找到可以依附的浮标，抓住救命稻草，有什么办法能让他逃离这悲惨的命运，继续将塞格琳留在他的生命中吗？

就在比洛多差点儿崩溃的时候，他突然灵机一动，想到个好主意。

要说这个主意还真是绝了，不仅是他独创的，而且充满灵性，想法也很大胆，连比洛多自己都吓了一跳，所以，他很快否决了这个想法。因为这个计划实在太疯狂了，而且荒诞得近乎有点危险，执行起来太冒险了，再说了，是否行得通还得两说。这种荒谬绝伦的主意怕是只有疯子才能想得出来，他应该第一时间把这样的主意扼杀在摇篮里，免得生出事端。为了分散注意力，比洛多再次拿起游戏手柄，继续猛烈攻击西昂星球的叛乱分子，但这个念头总是在他的脑海里挥之不去，无论他怎么做，这个想法还是总往外蹦，弄得比洛多实在厌倦了，不想再坚持了，他决心重新审视一遍这个计划。

也许这个主意并不是那么疯狂，虽然看起来很吓人，但更多的是心理上的恐惧，却并非天方夜谭。要说真的还有什么办法让他再次回到塞格琳身边，这恐怕是唯一可行的计划了。第二天，天刚露出鱼肚白，比洛多便抬起头，他明白已经别无选择，至少可以试一试。

第七章

窗户的缝隙被一块又厚实又粗糙的毛巾堵上了。比洛多全神贯注，听着隔壁房门和楼梯平台上的动静，目光在下面黑暗的小巷子里逡巡着，但并没有发现任何声响。他用力按压破碎的玻璃窗，玻璃碎片往里面掉落。比洛多一只手伸向破碎的洞口，找到门闩，从格朗普雷挨着小巷的公寓门里跳了进去，尔后飞快地把门关上。他进去了，搞定。

一股甜腻的酸臭味直冲鼻孔，原来他是在厨房里。他打开手电筒，往前走去，尽量踮着脚轻轻地走着，不让地板发出嘎吱嘎吱的声音。厨房既没有餐桌也没有椅子。那股怪味是吧台上发出来的，一包什么东西留在了那里，都腐烂了。可能是鱼。比洛多走过厨房，来到走廊，那里的地板铺着一层柔软的材料，不过并非一张剪裁合适的地毯，而是一张薄薄的类似床垫之类的东西，好像一直延伸到其他房间的地板上。走廊上一共有三扇门。第一扇门通往一间卧室，第二扇门则通往一个小小的洗手间，往前直走是起居室，那间房子被一个大屏风之类的东西分成两半。比洛多绕过一个形状奇特的矮雕塑，来到屏风的另一边，发现面前有一张写字台，边上则是一把带脚轮的扶手椅。在确定百叶窗是关上的后，他坐在了扶手椅上。

比洛多用手电筒射出的光束扫过写字台，发现上面有一台电脑，一本日历，几件小装饰物，一本字典，几支钢笔，还有好些纸张。他仔细看着那些纸，看来真是不虚此行，纸上面的笔迹无疑是格朗普雷本人的。他甚至在最上面的抽屉里有了更加令人兴奋的发现：死者写的俳句，得有整整一扎。在这些诗旁边，比洛多还发现了塞格琳的诗，这可是原版，他手里的都是复印的。还有她的照片呢！

比洛多抑制不住激动的心情，他喜欢这张笑脸，足以慰藉他的灵魂，她那如同杏仁一般的眼睛总是让他如坠梦中，他闻着塞格琳亲手抚摸过的幸运纸张，上面还残留着她的香水味，他忍不住亲吻起来。这种幸福的感觉虽然短暂，但冒这样的险算是值了。但比洛多的任务还没完成，他继续搜寻，在别的抽屉翻找着。他一心只想找到格朗普雷上一封信的草稿——就是那封被该死的下水道吞噬的信。他冒这么大的风险，最终目的也正是在此，可就在他准备搜寻的时候，突然听见门外有什么声音，有人在楼梯上讲话。比洛多吓得跳了起来，连忙关掉手电筒。是正在上楼的邻居发出的声响吗？还是警察前来抓捕这个可耻的盗窃犯?

比洛多可不想在这里坐以待毙，他把尽可能找到的纸张统统塞进了口袋里，打上门闩，冲到那个愚蠢的雕塑所在的起居室，从后门逃了出去，冲下楼梯，然后撒腿往小巷子的出口跑去，他足足跑了两个街区，直到确定后面没人追赶，才放慢脚步。他故作镇定，尽可能用最自然的姿势走路，以免引起人家的怀疑，但他的心如同擂鼓一样，怦怦地跳个不停。

入室盗窃的行为把他弄得满头大汗，比洛多好好洗了个澡。这会儿，他再次读起了塞格琳写的俳句，惊喜地发现这些俳句又恢复了生命力。跟着，他跟比尔偷偷合计后，又看了偷来的其他纸张，尤其是格朗普雷写的俳句，最终证实了他一直以来的怀疑，他们两个（曾经）确实是在切磋诗歌。格朗普雷的俳句看起来跟塞格琳的确有些不同，倒不是形式有所区别，而是意境。

时光若流水，
彷徨复彷徨，
恋恋崎岖礁石上。

浓浓的烟雾，

笼罩在上空，

城市得了肺气肿。

海水在激荡，

森林在摇晃，

地球，在低声吟唱。

兔子可不傻，

逃离了洞穴，

它不会坐以待毙。

冲破地平线，

往天地尽头眺望，

来迎接死亡。

　　跟塞格琳写的诗歌相比，格朗普雷的诗更加忧郁，也更富戏剧性，同样会引人共鸣：格朗普雷的俳句也会让你有种身临其境的感觉，不过揭露出来的东西更加昏暗。比洛多偷来的诗得有百来首。问题是这些诗都没有编号，也看不出诗歌完成的顺序，或者寄给塞格琳的顺序，哪里知道哪首俳句是最后一首——那首一直没寄到她手里的诗。

比洛多将塞格琳的原版照片放在他的床头柜上，他在黑暗中伸了伸懒腰，思忖着第一步计划完成后接下来该怎么办。继续第二步计划吗？他敢继续将这个疯狂的想法付诸行动吗？

比洛多睡着了，做了个奇怪的梦。他梦见了加斯顿·格朗普雷，他奄奄一息地躺在山毛榉大街的中央，那一幕就跟现实中的场景一模一样，只不过那个垂死之人似乎一点儿也不痛苦。相反，格朗普雷好像还很开心，甚至还朝比洛多眨了眨眼，像是认识他似的。

黎明时分，比洛多醒来的时候，决定继续执行他的计划。他给邮局打电话请了病假，这可是他五年来头一次，接下来，他甚至都没时间喝咖啡，而是埋头研究格朗普雷的手稿，模仿他的笔迹，比洛多之前的书法练习终于能派上用场了。

在仔细检查格朗普雷的笔迹后，比洛多很快发现一个不同寻常的特点——在所有的手稿中，有时候会在诗歌的正中间，出现一个特别的手绘符号。那是一个写得花里胡哨的圆，还是一个写得很有特色的字母 O？这个 O 有什么特殊的含义吗？写字的人似乎特别喜欢这个符号，到处都写了，看来比洛多只能猜测了。格朗普雷的书法倒挺有意思的，字写得落落大方。一笔一画遒劲有力，有棱有角，大胆结合了草书和印刷体的方式，力透纸背。要是比洛多的字也写得这么气势恢宏就好了。不过，他觉得自己倒也能模仿。他选了一支和格朗普雷所用的相同型号的圆珠笔，进行了第一次尝试，有模有样地模仿起了格朗普雷的几行诗。

临近中午的时候，他的第一个笔记本就写完了。比洛多在午餐时只吃了一罐沙丁鱼罐头，他站在一堆皱巴巴的草稿上，心不在焉地胡乱对付了一顿。吃完后，他继续练习，一直写到黄昏，要不是因为手抽筋，他还是不会休息的。比洛多揉着酸痛的手腕，灰心了一阵儿，也想过放弃，但他一想到在岛上翘首以盼的塞格琳，浑身就都有劲儿了，他便又拿起了笔，满怀决心地在纸上挥舞着。

天黑许久后，比洛多终于对自己的成绩感到满意了。他模仿格朗普雷笔迹的效果看起来还不错。这样一来，他的第二步计划算是成功了，但他并没有沾沾自喜，很快开始为接下来的挑战做准备，而即将面对的挑战难度要大多了。因为光会模仿人家的笔迹可不成，他还得知道怎么写诗。

之前比洛多没有刻意往这方面想，而是集中精力专注于技术方面的问题，但现在却不能再拖延了。能模仿格朗普雷的笔迹固然不错，但还得会像他一样写诗。现在，比洛多不得不闯入一片他未知的领域，进入全新的诗歌世界。他得使出浑身解数，写出让塞格琳眼前一亮的诗篇来。

可是比洛多根本就没能力揣摩别人的语言，等到天亮的时候，他也就想出了"水"这个字，这还是受塞格琳那首婴儿游泳的俳句启发。他实在想不出任何隽言妙语来了。当然，他还可以给这个词加上不同的修饰语，比如说：清澈的水、流动的水、静止的水。可这玩意儿能叫诗吗？他整个早上都处于恍惚的状态中，绞尽脑汁地想在水上做点文章，让这个词可以脱胎换骨：消防水、自来水、苏打水？

水源？

他打算先打个盹儿再说，结果梦见自己溺水了，幸好及时醒来了，好好吸了几口气，继续对着空白的稿纸。洗碗水？圣水？水甲虫？水厂？

跳入水中?

在水面上行走?

  这时,他看到比尔乐此不疲地在浴缸里转来转去,终于提笔写下:"水中的鱼儿。"这行字恰好有五个音节,他的诗算是完成了三分之一。

  但是,比洛多很快用挑剔的眼光看着这几个字,随即把它们划掉了。

  这句话总共五个字,就没有一个让他满意的。照这个速度,怕是等到圣诞节他都写不完。

  他真得加快速度才行。他要怎样才能成为一个诗人呢?比洛多心里想。这能学得会吗?兴许有一种叫作俳句入门的课程呢?可是黄页上也没有记录有这么一家教授诗歌的学校。现在情况这么急,该向谁求助呢?日本大使馆吗?现在,至少有一件事已经很明确了:比洛多必须赶鸭子上架,更多地了解有关俳句的知识了。

第八章

　　比洛多在中央图书馆的日本文学区搜寻，发现了几本极具价值的书，没用多长时间他就了解了平常不好意思找人打听的俳句知识。其实俳句的规则非常简单，同时达到一种刹那永恒的意境。一首优秀的俳句要涉及自然元素（日语称为季语）或是包含非人类独有的特征。俳句的语言既要言简意赅，同时又要兼具复杂、精妙的特点，要避免使用押韵和比喻这种惯用的文学手法。俳句好比是一张快照、一张细节图。可能是人们生活中的某个片段、某段回忆、某个梦境，却也实实在在的是一首诗，能够吸引人的感官，而不从思想上说教。

　　比洛多逐渐明白其中的奥秘了，他甚至明白塞格琳和格朗普雷书信交往中的俳句所具有的特殊意义。他们的这种行为称为连歌，这项传统要追溯至中世纪日本皇室举行的文学比赛。

　　比洛多像是捡到了宝，迫不及待地想跟人谈谈，于是，他把他的发现告诉了罗伯特，还给他读了芭蕉、芜村和一茶写的著名俳句，但俳句中的不易和流行之间的微妙平衡，也就是超越人类的永恒和稍纵即逝之间的关系很难被他的这位同事理解，他觉得这样的诗歌没什么意义，顶多算是一种复杂的精神自慰。倒不是说罗伯特对日本文学存有偏见。相反，他承认自己对日本漫画情有独钟，尤其喜欢那种性变态的漫画，他以前曾竭力向比洛多推荐过，还拿了一本给他看。

现在比洛多了解了不少俳句的知识，很想找一个志同道合的人聊聊，便找到了塔尼娅。起初，那个年轻的女侍应并没有表现出特别的兴趣，因为当时是玛德琳诺餐厅最忙的时候。比洛多给她看了一本名为《十七世纪传统俳句》的书，那可是他从图书馆借来的珍藏本，读者可以一睹古日语俳句的风采，可女孩的眼里并没有出现他所期盼的热切目光。塔尼娅承认这些诗写得很美，也很玄妙，充满神秘主义色彩。比洛多深表同意。结合表意文字和表音假名，再加上日语独特的书写方式，俳句的美被展现得淋漓尽致，甚至连那种不可名状的意境也能表达出来。

可爱的金鱼，

摆动着鱼鳍，

鱼缸里吐着泡泡。

这样的文字会有诗意吗？比洛多第一次觉得他悟出里面的门道了，还有什么比金鱼更能代表日本呢？但是，现在他也没那么肯定了。不过，他感觉自己的方向是对的，也能体会到俳句所推崇的特点：轻盈、真实、客观，热爱这世界所有的生物。但是，俳句所描写的事物本身不应该具备让人推崇的特征吗？他虽然很尊敬比尔，但一条鱼真的适合被表达得诗情画意吗？于是，比洛多开始在脑海里搜寻更能体现诗意的动物，他随即想到了鸟，这种动物的确具有"轻盈"的特征。

> 湛蓝的天空，
>
> 鸟儿立在天线上，
>
> 啾啾地叫着。

这首诗比那首以鱼为主题的诗真的要好吗？比洛多不免为自己的平庸感到沮丧，他刚刚建立的自信又慢慢消失了。了解俳句在理论上应该包含什么内容是一回事，自己能不能写出来又是另外一回事。

而且，文学素养才是问题的关键：先不管这些诗歌的艺术价值，不管是有关鱼的俳句还是有关鸟的俳句，它们看起来都不像格朗普雷所写，这才是这两首诗最根本的问题。最重要的是，他必须写一首打上格朗普雷烙印的诗。比洛多必须揣摩出那位死者内心的想法，这样塞格琳才不会起疑。

　　比洛多突然想到，他可能得从分析格朗普雷的笔迹开始，在笔相学方面好好做做文章。于是，他还专门找了一本相关的书。比洛多很快获悉，这门学科主要是经验的积累，只能通过熟能生巧达成目的。他也不大确定自己能否在这么短的时间内了解格朗普雷的性格。晚上，他待在电视机前看书的时候，注意力却被一名演员的评论给吸引了，此人被邀请来讲述自己的职业生涯，解释他是如何演绎一名去世多年的国家元首。这位演员提到他先是从模仿伟人的小动作开始，比如对方一些怪癖、行为方式、生活习惯，逐渐了解他性格的内在特质，从而充分了解个人。比洛多大喜，合上了那本笔相学的书，他觉得刚才听到的那席话才是关键，让他有了希望。

　　第二天，比洛多来到玛德琳诺餐厅，没有坐在他以前经常落座的吧台前面，而是坐在了格朗普雷经常坐的长凳上，还叫了那位死者喜欢的食物。塔尼娅把番茄三明治端到他面前的时候，很是不解。比洛多一边吃着三明治，一边坐在新位置上欣赏周围陌生的景色，不光是餐厅里面的，还有街边的景色。

吃过午饭后，他继续自己的工作，不过仍然不忘模仿格朗普雷。他会仔细观察周围的世界，不会放过任何能给他的俳句创作带来素材的事件和细节。比如，毛毛虫爬过人行道，纵横交错的树叶如同大网一样悬挂在街道上，松鼠在公园的长凳下你追我赶，风吹着粉红色的长裤在晾衣绳上翻飞，这样的场景可能成为诗的素材吗？

比洛多来到山毛榉大街，悠闲地在街上散步，尽量以格朗普雷的眼光看待周遭的一切，尽量揣摩他的内心去感同身受。比洛多正准备进入那间无人居住的公寓，去感受那人真正的内心世界时，他突然找到了一条真正的途径：一张广告。

那是一张红底黑字的广告，用透明胶带贴在窗户上，上面写着：此屋出租。

比洛多在一个很小的菜园里找到了公寓的主人。那是一个穿着考究、疑心重重的女人，看到比洛多穿的制服时，她似乎放心了不少。这位叫布洛楚的女人随即放下了手中的活计，领着比洛多来到公寓的三层，让他进了公寓，这一次，比洛多倒可以光明正大地进去了。跟天黑时偷偷进来相比，在光天化日之下进入那里的感觉有点奇怪。跟之前留下的坏印象比较，现在这间屋子光线充足，给人一种愉悦的感觉，典型的日式装潢风格令屋子很是特别。上次进来的时候，比洛多并没有发现这一点，因为手电筒的光线本就不亮，他只看了个大概，再加上紧张，感觉什么都是蓝绿色的，所以他并没有发现里面的家具、百叶窗、台灯，几乎所有的家具都被打上了日式风格的烙印。让人有种突然来到旭日之国的错觉。

比洛多四下看了看，看到不少奇形怪状的盆栽，一台打字机，一件装饰物，几件雕塑——一个懒洋洋的艺伎，一个笑容狡黠的矮胖僧人，还有个怒气冲冲，挥舞着长剑的日本武士。之前比洛多踩在上面，好奇是什么材质的地毯其实是榻榻米垫子，那东西如同巨大的拼图一块块在地板上拼接起来，而他上次慌不择路撞翻的奇怪物体，其实是一张用昂贵的木材打造的漂亮小桌子，做工相当精致，雕成向叶柄弯曲的树叶形状，八成被当成了茶几。写字台的两侧则是房子里仅有的西式设计风格，那里有一个高高的书架，上面塞满了书。起居室则被一张可折叠的纸屏风一分为二，屏风上是一幅山间樱花盛开的风景画，另一边则用作餐室，那里只有一张低矮的桌子，周围则是刺绣的垫子，其中一张垫子上端有一座禅宗风格的小花园。

　　卧室的装修则比较简单，里面仅有一个蒲团和一个衣柜，衣柜装有活动门，门上镶嵌着全身镜。洗手间里有一个形状奇特的小木盆，盆里还有一个又高又扁的大木桶，显然是用来排水的。

　　看来格朗普雷对日本的生活方式有着强烈的兴趣，难怪他会这么痴迷俳句，而那件他从不脱下的鲜红色睡袍显然是一件和服，现在可能被丢在衣柜某个阴暗的角落里，或是跟主人一起火化了。

　　厨房的吧台一尘不染，之前腐烂的味道也没有了——想必是布洛楚夫人清理过了。门上破碎的玻璃也已换成了新的，没有任何迹象表明最近房子里进过贼。这时，布洛楚夫人稍显慌张地解释：她得知房子的前一任租户在遗嘱里将所有的家具和私人物品都留给她时，感到非常吃惊，想来是因为这个房客没有子嗣，也没有近亲。这种情况对她来说很是不便，因为她必须自己花费时间和金钱处理掉这些物品。但这对比洛多而言可是天大的好事，他当即表示可以按照房子现有的样子，原封不动地租下公寓，布洛楚夫人大喜过望，欣然接受了。几分钟后，比洛多当场签下租赁合约，拿到了新家的钥匙。

　　比洛多内心甭提有多开心了，他相信这下准能写出好诗了。

现在，他可以亲自在格朗普雷待过的地方，按照他平日里的饮食起居生活了。如果真要想探究格朗普雷的内心世界，还有比这更好的法子吗？比洛多在公寓的每间房子里走来走去，他兴奋得不能自已，直到对房子的细节都了然于心。他仔细检查里面的每一件物品，让自己沉浸在房间的整体气氛中，忘情地闻着各种物品散发出来的气味。比洛多像吸血鬼一样嗅着房间的前主人留在墙上的气息，寻找有关他的一切线索，直到对他的内心世界了如指掌，按照他的思维方式去思考、作诗。

第九章

比洛多没有在格朗普雷的壁橱里发现骷髅，也没有在他的冰箱里发现可疑的物品，橱柜里也没有什么古怪离奇的东西，除了不少茶叶和几瓶日本米酒外，再没有惹人注意的东西了。不过，他在衣柜的抽屉和洗衣篮里发现许多不成对的袜子，他寻思这些臭烘烘的东西能否让他一窥死者的内心世界。难不成格朗普雷有从自助洗衣店里偷袜子的癖好？这些袜子都是他收集的吗？难道他会在满月的时候变成蜈蚣吗？除了这些，屋子里再也没异乎寻常的东西。

但最让比洛多吃惊的还是书架上的那些书，当然，大部分都是日本作家的作品，足足有好几百本，就连作者的名字和书名都充满了异域风情。他随便打开了一位叫山岛的作者写的小说，看到一段这样的描写，一个年轻的女人从自己的乳房里挤出奶，滴在爱人的茶杯里。比洛多被书中怪异的描写搅得很是不安，便赶紧合上了书，决定过段时间再去了解日本文学，现在还是继续研究上回夜闯格朗普雷住处时没来得及带走的纸稿。

他正是这个时候发现了塞格琳的一封信，那是一封普普通通的信，通篇都是叙述性的文体，是三年前写的，那也是瓜德罗普岛的女人第一次给格朗普雷写信，她在信中声称自己是日本诗歌的爱好者，对格朗普雷在一本文学刊物上发表的评述小林一茶俳句的文章大加赞赏，他们也就是从那个时候开始通信的。因为他们志趣相投，两人的关系发展得很快，过了一阵儿，在格朗普雷的提议下，两人就这样，你来我往互相寄诗给对方。他们就是这样相识相熟的，对日本文化的共同爱好拉近了他们的距离，使他们成了朋友。比洛多至少解开了一个谜题。

第一个谜题解决后，比洛多决定再试着写写诗。因为那天是周五，他整个周末都有时间，于是，他决定把自己锁在家里，拉上百叶窗，向那些俳句大师祈祷，虔诚地希望他们能够赐予他写诗的天赋。接下来，他就像那些采珠者一样，一头扎了进去，在自己的精神世界里徜徉。

比洛多认为，他先前的俳句缺少的是"不易"的主题，也就是少了对永恒的探索。这天，他琢磨了整整一个晚上，酝酿写一首歌颂黎明壮丽景色的诗，只用了短短几个小时就完成了。

太阳升起了，

像金色的大气球，

爬上地平线。

比洛多觉得写得还行，里面包含了许多永恒的主题，但怎么看都缺少"流行"的元素，也就是所谓刹那或者世俗的东西。比洛多希望他的俳句能将这两种元素完美地结合起来，这才是优秀的俳句。于是，他又开始琢磨起来，必须想方设法完美地融合这两种矛盾的元素。

太阳升起了，

我把奶酪片，

放在奶油吐司上。

太阳升起了，

如金色肚脐，

悬在空空的肚上。

太阳升起了，

似金色奶酪，

我们一起吃早餐。

　　这时，比洛多听到肚子咕噜噜叫起来。这没什么奇怪的，他已经一整天没吃东西了，一直在埋头创作。他在想，一种事情是否能被另一种事情所解释？诗歌和饿肚子是一回事吗？比洛多暂时没去想这个问题，他去了本地一家名为"东方美味"的日式料理店吃了午饭。

　　下午晚些的时候，布洛楚夫人到家中做客，还带来了一篮子水果，算是欢迎他的礼物。夫人之前就已经留意到他一下儿就把家安顿好了，还一直提醒他把东西都捎上，千万别落了。比洛多自然不愿意放过了解格朗普雷的任何机会，他把夫人留了下来，在那个漂亮的叶片状的茶几旁招待她喝茶。礼貌地寒暄几句后，比洛多便将话题引到了那位前租客的身上。他回忆了格朗普雷惨死的场景，发表了一番评论，对死者进行了哀悼。比洛多获悉格朗普雷曾在附近的一所大学教文学，尽管他很年轻，但前几年就退休了。布洛楚夫人见比洛多对格朗普雷兴趣浓厚，便透露说这个可怜的人最近几个月行为古怪——几乎没离开过公寓，一遍遍地播放中国音乐唱片，她当时就在想这人可能要崩溃了，还曾偷偷说过他可能会死这类的话。

布洛楚夫人离开后，比洛多一边清洗茶壶，一边想着刚才的话。关于格朗普雷的性格，在很多方面仍然是一团迷雾，他的思想也复杂得很，大部分人都不了解，但比洛多已经看到了曙光。布洛楚夫人先前的谈话给了他一个新的线索：音乐。比洛多暂时还不清楚这个线索是否能让他更多地了解那人，他马上开始在格朗普雷的唱片中翻找起来，很快发现了女房东提到的中国音乐，其实是传统的日本音乐。他随便选了一张，放在唱片机上。忧郁动听的笛声和拨弄琵琶弦的声音从唱片上缓缓流出，美妙的音乐声顿时在房间内响起。比洛多突然来了灵感，拿起手中的笔……

他一遍一遍地放着唱片，一边大口喝着茶，一边写诗，虚无的时光就这样悄悄地溜走了。十三弦古筝奏出美妙的弦音，同时伴随三弦琴尖锐的声音，有时是口琴，笙箫发出的声音犹如天籁，女人的哼唱声也叫人如痴如醉。比洛多写诗的时候像是深陷恍惚中，竭力达到一种"侘"（即指跟自然和谐共处的状态下生出的超凡脱俗的美），沉浸于古老的"寂"（朴素、平静、孤独）之美。他想象着自己在深秋时节徜徉在红叶纷飞的皇家山，满山慵懒、一点儿也不知道羞耻的树木，树叶在瑟瑟秋风中发出沙沙的声音，鸟儿即将离别，昆虫最后一次发出嘎吱嘎吱的声响，他想将这些景色呈现在自己的笔下。

他绞尽脑汁地寻找合适的词继续写着，想趁文字消失之前将其写在纸上，如同用纸做的网捕捉蝴蝶一样。他时常会想到某句自己勉强还算满意的句子，但五分钟后就觉得这句话索然无味了，只得把它扔到废纸篓中。接下来他又会重新写过，在一堆皱巴巴的废纸中来回踱步，偶尔也会休息一下，在那座禅宗风格的小花园的沙地里写写画画，也许还会重新读一遍格朗普雷或者塞格琳写的俳句，他会大声读出来，两人的心有灵犀让他艳羡不已。

他从"东方美味"餐厅叫来了寿司，趁比尔没注意的时候才小心翼翼地吃了，然后又继续写了一整晚的诗，地上全是白花花的草稿纸，礼拜天又写了整整一天，光是喝了点日本米酒，然后又折腾了一个晚上，直到弄得自己头昏脑涨，眼睛都眯成一条缝了。最后，他的笔从指间滑落，他一头栽倒在蒲团上，昏昏沉沉地睡了过去，梦见的全是栩栩如生的象形文字，还梦见塞格琳解开上衣，从乳房里挤出一点乳汁，滴在他的双唇之间……

周一早上醒来后，他感觉脑袋上的神经像擂鼓一样，不停地悸动着，他一口气吞了四片阿司匹林，洗澡洗了很久，然后在几张侥幸没被撕碎的稿纸中挑选，最后选了一张描写暮光的诗：

太阳落山了，

在阳台上打哈欠，

窗边打呼噜。

这首三行俳句还有点诗歌的味道，比洛多心想，而且跟格朗普雷的诗歌比起来，也不算差得太远。这首诗看起来还成，但还是不够好，他整整齐齐地将这张纸撕成极小的碎片，大手一甩，纸片像雪花一样纷纷落下。不到两个礼拜，他第二次向邮局请假。比洛多在家里泡了热茶，又继续埋头写诗，他决心已下，九头牛也拉不回了。

临近中午的时候，邮筒"嘭"地响了一声，把比洛多吓了一大跳，他心里不免有些妒忌，看来找个人取代他的工作并非难事，跟着，他下楼取走了格朗普雷的信，其中两封是广告单，一封是账单，还有一封塞格琳写来的信。

比洛多兴奋得不能自已。这事完全出乎了他的意料。他从没想过塞格琳在格朗普雷尚未回复她的俳句时居然又寄来了一封信。他颤抖地用裁纸刀打开信封，跟平日里一样，里面只有一张纸：

令你失望了？

忘了这秋日，

友谊还如往常吗？

这首俳句坦诚、直白的风格让比洛多深受刺激，字里行间明显透露出来的焦虑也让他大为惊慌。看来塞格琳习惯了这位笔友的准时，没有收到回信让她忧心忡忡。这个可怜的女人还担心可能惹他生气了。比洛多想象着她在写信时的忐忑不安，漂亮的脸上写满了焦虑，塞格琳美丽的容颜会变得憔悴。一想到塞格琳的样子，比洛多不由得心如刀割。他觉得自己必须抓紧时间行动，得赶紧写一封信来安慰她，让灿烂的笑容重新回到她脸上。比洛多不能再拖拖拉拉了，反正得将那首该死的俳句寄出去。

第 十 章

　　加斯顿·格朗普雷新坟的空隙处慢慢冒出一层青草。比洛多仍在冥思苦想。希望这位死者能给他带来些许灵感，也许能从他仍在游荡的灵魂中得到启发。他静静地在脑海中描绘塞格琳焦虑的心情，想到时间已经非常紧迫了，他一再安慰自己他的初衷是好的，对塞格琳的感情也是真诚的。比洛多老老实实地告诉沉睡在地下的那个男人，他在模仿其作品的时候费尽了心血，虔诚地祈祷格朗普雷能给他启发：他到底该怎么做？他还要采取什么样的行动？还要做出什么牺牲？他还要怎样做才能找到打开诗歌殿堂的钥匙？

　　比洛多跪在湿漉漉的草地上，等待着，聚精会神地听着，但那座坟墓没有给他任何启示，也没有任何阴森森的回应。很显然，那个死人不会给人任何意见，不过……

　　日有所思，夜有所梦，墓地走过一遭后，比洛多当晚就梦见了格朗普雷。他梦见自己醒了过来，发现格朗普雷穿着那件红色的和服，站在他的床前。虽然他苍白的眉毛和蓬乱的头发上还有斑斑血迹，但化身为鬼的格朗普雷脸上却一直挂着笑，他的脚上像装有滚珠，在房间里穿梭着。他走到衣橱那儿，打开门，指了指最上面的架子……

　　比洛多一下醒了过来，至少他觉得自己醒了，也许是陷入了更深层的梦中，他在想到底是梦见自己醒了，还是真的醒了？他发现格朗普雷的鬼魂已经不见了，他还是倾向于第二种判断。他看着衣橱，不知道那个鬼为什么会指着架子上面，他百思不得其解。这当然只是一场梦啦，但比洛多的好奇心占了上风，他决定走到近前一探究竟，说不定那里真有什么东西。最上面的架子又高又深，比洛多伸手，指尖在里面摸索着，他摸到了什么东西，最里头藏有一个盒子。他吃了一惊，把盒子拉了出来，原来是个黑色的纸盒，很大，不是很重，上面印着日语。比洛多把盒子放在床上，揭开盒盖。发现薄棉纸里面是一件被折得整整齐齐的红色和服。

　　那件和服看起来没人穿过。比洛多从盒子里把衣服拿出来展开，衣服是闪光的丝质面料，非常漂亮。比洛多忍不住穿在身上。让他吃惊的是，非常合身。他走了几步，又转了几圈，想看看这件和服有多轻盈。他甩动下摆，感觉像阿拉伯的劳伦斯第一次穿酋长服的样子。比洛多对着镜子好好欣赏了一番。

那件衣服非常合身，简直是为他量身定做的。比洛多像是被电击了，感觉一股细细的电流从他的神经流过，让他全身有种刺痛的感觉。

他突然灵机一动，跑出卧室，来到起居室，坐在办公桌旁，将一张空白的纸放在面前，拿起一支笔，任笔尖停留在纸上。然后奇迹发生了。那只圆珠笔的笔尖开始在纸上划过，画出类似地震仪才能画出的线条。比洛多还是在做梦吗？他突然有了灵感，那感觉像是内心的堤坝突然决了口，又像熄火的引擎终于发动了起来。一张张画面向他脑海袭来，像台球一样互相撞击着，几乎令他应接不暇。

一分钟后，一切结束了，比洛多终于不再感觉到那股神秘的力量，他只觉得像是虚脱了。眼前是一首俳句。那首诗是自动生成的，一气呵成，没有删改一个字，而且那笔迹绝对是格朗普雷的：

高高的山上，

雪终年不化，

一如我们的友谊。

比洛多试图弄明白刚才到底发生了什么事，他觉得这很可能是一种条件反射，那件他找到的和服成了催化剂。那件衣服好比格朗普雷的皮囊，数日来他一直在苦苦创作，穿上那件和服激发了他的创作灵感，说不定那件衣服有灵性呢？要么就是格朗普雷想满足他的愿望，想帮他，他被灵魂短暂地附体了？比洛多一时拿不定主意。但最要紧的就是那首诗了。不管是不是被灵魂附体了，反正比洛多刚才写的那首俳句肯定是他这辈子写得最好的了。不过，这首诗能否让塞格琳感到满意呢？她会喜欢吗？

　　比洛多把纸折好，放进信封里。可就在他准备封上信封的时候，却犹豫了，还有最后一个细节，他很是纠结。要不要在俳句上加那个圆圈呢？格朗普雷每次都会画个圈圈。说不定这是他的签名，或者类似印章的效果，要是没有画，兴许会引起人家的怀疑。他得再看看死者以前的信才能弄明白。想到这儿，丢了格朗普雷最后一封信再次让他感觉特别懊恼，比洛多本来已经没想这件事了。他封上信封，很快投递了出去，免得再改变主意。

　　估摸着要等上五六天，塞格琳才能收到这首俳句，而收到她的回信大概要花费同样多的时间，前提是她没有怀疑这封信，愿意回信，如果真是这样的情况，那他的计划就算是成功了。

十一天后，比洛多终于收到了回信。他盼星星盼月亮，终于把那封信盼来了。他不停地祈祷，一直不敢碰那支笔，也不敢穿上那件和服，生怕会破坏命运微妙的平衡，但那封信最终还是来了，现在就在他的手中。他一动不动地站在分理处的柜台旁，迫不及待地冲到洗手间，把自己锁在最后一个隔间里，撕开信封，读起来：

　　　　　高耸的山峰，
　　　　来自谦卑登山者，
　　　　　尊敬的朝拜。

比洛多一下子被带到了《丁丁在西藏》那本书中描绘的喜马拉雅山中的场景。他紧紧抓住岩石，站在一处山坡陡峭的半山腰上，四周都是洁白无瑕的雪，火辣的阳光晃得人炫目。他面前的山峰高耸入云，虽然隔得很远，但在稀薄的空气中像是触手可及似的，映衬在深蓝色的天空下，轮廓分外清晰，崎岖的山体给人一种喜怒无常、盛气凌人的感觉。

等到比洛多慢慢欣赏完塞格琳的诗歌，他一下儿觉得精神为之一振，感觉自己跟雪人一样强壮，好比是大出血后输入了新鲜的血液。他的计划成功了！她相信了！

第十一章

峻峭的高山，

私底下希望，

有人来征服它们。

它们勇敢地，

炫耀雪崩的外衣，

心却很柔弱。

山惧怕黑夜，

孤独地哭泣，

泪水汇成了瀑布。

所以湖才会，

冰冷地趴在山间，

体会那寂寥。

比洛多感觉幸福极了，真是夫复何求，那件和服就挂在衣橱里，随时可以派上用场。不过，他尽量避免经常使用它，要省着点用才行，因此，他每次只会在回复塞格琳的时候才会穿。他只需要把这件具有魔法的衣服穿在身上，他的灵魂就会长上翅膀，振翅高飞，色彩和幻象会一股脑向他袭来。比洛多不愿意用超自然现象来解释这件事。他认为在梦见格朗普雷的鬼魂后发现和服只是巧合，只能说自己太幸运了，至于接下来的事，完全是潜意识的功劳。再说了，他也不打算继续纠缠这事，因为他担心太好奇了，会影响他创作的势头，到时候怕写不出好的诗歌来。奇迹到底是怎样产生的对他来说并不重要，只要管用就行。他可以一直给塞格琳写信，只要他能梦见她在潺潺的小溪旁吹着笛子，像卢梭的画里一样逗着蛇玩，在绿油油的草地上打着瞌睡，鲜艳的野花将她围在当中，森林里的动物争先恐后地守卫在她身旁，他就心满意足了。

微亮的晨曦，
悄悄睁开睫毛，瞧
闪亮的舞台。

孤 独 邮 差

水果贩的头发上，
　那飞舞的花，
　　居然是蝴蝶。

万圣节那天晚上，
　小怪兽出没，
　　在人行道上。

　马儿在奔跑，
　看来很慌张，
不知什么咬了它。

　水洼似水晶，
脚下的草嘎吱响，
　　冬天又来了。

　大猫咕噜叫，
老鼠在眼皮底下，
　　仓皇逃跑了。

最无瑕的美，

柔软的雪花，

自然的鬼斧神工。

巨大的黑背，

在乘风破浪，

是抹香鲸在嬉戏。

　　她游啊游啊，嬉戏玩乐，她身形巨大，却动作轻灵。她的肤色黝黑，流线型的曲线优美动人，在洒满阳光的海面上非常显眼。她掠过闪闪发光的水面，有时候会把背部露出来。她游来游去，发出悦耳的声音，她的歌声在大海上回荡，因为她是一头鲸鱼。他也是一头鲸鱼。两个人化身成了鲸鱼，在一起遨游，并肩游向远方。那个地方没有名字，只是被称为"远方"，就在这片浩瀚蓝色海域的远处。他们悠然自得，徐徐前行，在柔和的晨曦光线下，轻快地游着。他们会去打猎，然后，他们将乘风破浪，继续前进。他们时不时浮出水面，喷出一道道含有碘化蒸汽的水柱，让他们的肺中充满空气，他们在浪潮间轻轻地摆动，漂了一段时间，然后，他们再次潜入平静的水下。

孤 独 邮 差

当一头鲸鱼，感觉好极了。和她在一起，只和她在一起，自由自在地并排遨游，是那么美妙的体验。如果他有选择，他宁愿自己是这片汪洋，那样一来，他就可以更加亲密地将塞格琳拥入怀中，无论何时何地，他都可以张开无尽的怀抱拥抱她，永远轻抚她的皮肤，但即便如此，当一头鲸鱼，也是那样美好。只要有她陪在身边，他就能获得极大的快乐，携手追寻永恒的时光。

此时，她忽然叫了一声，一头扎进水里，逃离刺目的光线。她是不是发现了可口的猎物？她是为了追求在海底探索的乐趣，去陌生的沉船残骸探险一番，抑或，她是在玩捉迷藏？他跟在她后面，用强有力的尾巴划水，猛冲过去，他不要落在后面。他跟着她钻进水中，被幽暗的海水包围，大海的拥抱越来越紧，也越来越冰冷。他看不到她，却能感觉到她在无边的海水中游动而产生的震颤，他听到她在附近黑暗的海水中唱歌。她是在呼唤。她是在呼唤他，他用歌声回应，因为身为鲸鱼，这就是他们交流的方式：在虚无的海洋中歌唱，无惧于黑暗幽深的大海。

第 十 二 章

孩童在呼叫，
不住挥动手中棒，
　一分到手了。

女孩惊声叫，
瞧见了一只蜈蚣，
　趴在窗台上。

院中晾衣裳，
洗净衣物都冻僵，
　麻雀直哆嗦。

芳邻叫艾梅，
穿着花裙养花儿，
　帮她浇浇水。

孤独邮差

时值一月，逼人的严寒到处肆虐。一晃，比洛多搬进格朗普雷的公寓已有三个月了。他住得很舒服，完全把这里当成了家，却也还是觉得自己住在"格朗普雷的公寓"。这是他的潜意识，但也表示他非常尊重格朗普雷，正是格朗普雷带给了他很多欢乐。他只是在合适的时候才会返回他以前的住处，取走为数不多的给他的邮件，而且，不断有乌七八糟的信息涌进他的语音信箱，他只好把它们都删除。他的家具和大部分物品都在原处。他其实只拿了很少的几样东西去格朗普雷的公寓，免得破坏那里令人愉快的东方氛围。

他不会再住原本的公寓了，本可以将其转租他人，但他并没有这么做，因为他用得着那里的地址，既可以用来做掩护，又可以让他继续在山毛榉大街享受宁静的平行生活。如此一来，他一方面不必担心不速之客的到来，另一方面也不用再面对罗伯特不合时宜地找上门来。比洛多一直瞒着罗伯特，光是想到罗伯特穿着巨大的木屐，出现在他这个幽静的日式风格的避难所中，打扰他的隐居，他就情不自禁地发抖。

罗伯特又不是傻子，自然产生了怀疑。比洛多一直不接电话，他去比洛多的家，也发现已人去楼空，他就知道事情有古怪。罗伯特问这问那，搞得比洛多非常尴尬，而且，比洛多发现越来越难避开那些问题。

除了罗伯特好管闲事，总打听比洛多的事儿，外界很少对他的隐居生活横加干涉，他也可以只专注于他想象出来的爱情。玛德琳诺餐厅的女招待塔尼娅从不错过任何机会打探他对日本诗歌的研究进展。

事实上，比洛多早就习惯了利用吃完甜点之后的午休时间修改他送给塞格琳的俳句。塔尼娅大感不解，经常问他都写了什么，能不能给她见识见识。他只好尽可能地婉转拒绝，假称那些俳句是隐秘的东西，但年轻的女招待依然对他的作品展现出了浓烈的兴趣，这倒叫他不免动容。一次次拒绝塔尼娅，他不由得心有愧疚。他希望能讨她的喜欢，便承诺以后会专门为她写一首俳句。她听了非常兴奋。

此外，比洛多几乎并不与其他人交往。他偶尔和布洛楚夫人寒暄几句，但最近发生了一件事，导致他们之间的交流就更少了：有一天，她来敲他的门，请他把中国音乐的音量调小一点，但看到他穿着格朗普雷的和服，这个女人露出了震惊的表情。那之后，她就没那么热情了，而且，还会用狐疑的目光打

孤 独 邮 差

量比洛多。他觉得这也是可以理解的。在外人看来，他的行为的确是令人诧异。就算是在他自己看来，按照别人的思想思考，穿别人的衣服，确实是怪异至极。但他完全接受他自己在这方面的古怪行为，全然不在乎别人的想法。关键在于不要失去内心深处的理智。

拂晓的长凳，
人们发现流浪汉，
被活活冻死。

苏弗雷火山，
山顶处云雾缭绕，
似崇高思想。

自天堂吹落，
漫天飞舞的雪花，
积雪三十厘。

纵情跳舞吧，

嘉年华王在燃烧，

畅饮杯中酒。

　　在克里奥尔语中，vidé 是游行、队列之意，在瓜德罗普岛，二月末也是举办狂欢节的时间。Touloulou 是一种舞蹈，跳这种舞蹈的时候，女士可以优先选择舞伴，Vaval 则是嘉年华之王，是当地的福神，有点像雪人博纳。Grand brilé 是一种很受欢迎的仪式，在圣灰星期三的夜间举行。在嘉年华的最后，伴随着众人歇斯底里的哭喊声，烧掉不幸的嘉年华之王。至于可以流动的 ti-punch，它是什么意思则显而易见了。比洛多觉得这和魁北克狂欢节差不多，只是这里的温度要高出华氏五十度。

　　他急于和塞格琳分享他的欢乐心情，并且告诉她，他家乡的狂欢节与她岛上的嘉年华都很喜庆，他送给她一首俳句：

让舞伴转圈，

先生们统统后退，

女孩跳起来。

他从未踏足过舞池，那天夜里，他梦到他快乐地与塞格琳旋转舞动，他们身在一个小镇里，镇子位于魁北克古城区和皮特尔角之间，气氛喜庆，看起来很不一样。他还梦到他们在优维尔广场结冰的路面上疯狂地跳利戈顿舞，过了一会儿，他又梦到他们在芳香闷热的胜利广场，激情四射地跳着戈卡舞。塞格琳笑着舞着，不知疲倦，她的一头秀发在夜色中甩动着。

第 十 三 章

　　三月的第一个礼拜一，一个包裹从法国寄来给加斯顿·格朗普雷，里面装着一份名叫《禅圆》的手稿，创作者就是格朗普雷本人，封面插图上画的是一个黑色圆圈，圆圈外沿参差不齐。又是这个神秘的圆，在已故格朗普雷的所有书信上都有这个圆圈。

　　除了手稿，还有一封短信，是巴黎芦苇出版社自由体诗歌的编辑所写的。编辑先是称赞这部作品颇有水准，但很遗憾不能将其出版。

　　比洛多翻看了这部只有六十来页的手稿，每一页上都有一首俳句，看到那首熟悉的开场诗，他并不惊讶：

时光若流水，

彷徨复彷徨，

恋恋崎岖礁石上。

　　接下来的一首俳句也很熟悉，他都读过很多遍了，有时候，有的版本与眼前这一版有些许不同：

孤 独 邮 差

东方的海鸥，

凄厉尖叫似女巫，

在午夜狂啸。

花岗岩叠嶂，

云杉树交错缠结，

长长的海滩。

高尔夫球手，

完美地一挥，

多么漂亮的胜利。

他驾驭着光，

将球送入高空中，

与星辰辉映。

比洛多以前一直是从格朗普雷的混乱手稿中随机挑出俳句来看，但现在，按照作者排列的特定顺序看来，则是一种极为不同的体验。照此读来，诗句犹如拥有了魔力。比洛多翻着手稿，感觉他正在前往一个隐秘的目的地，仿佛他在情不自禁地向无情的命运前进。那些俳句彼此之间产生共鸣，在人的心中创造出了动人节奏，久久萦绕不去。看了这些俳句，他竟然觉得似曾相识，感觉好像看过或是梦到过它们。它们激起了沉淀在他记忆深处的古老影像。

深邃的大海，
幽暗至极云墨色，
光亮被扼杀。

胸腔无一物，
食尸者掏空一切，
成为了主宰。

冲破地平线，
往天地尽头眺望，
来迎接死亡。

> 深海的王子，
>
> 快乐美人鱼，成对，
>
> 回到你身旁。

　　这些俳句虽阴郁却也泛着光辉，犹如排成队列漂浮在海上的鱼儿一样发出的磷光。这本诗集的名字让比洛多迷惑不解，他在字典中查过，却找不到"禅圆"这个词。他又去网上找，满意地看到屏幕上出现了很多解释，每个解释里的圆都和封面上的那个差不多，他还发现这是禅宗佛教的一个传统标志。禅圆代表心灵虚空，这样人就可以开悟。数千年来，禅宗法师都在画这个圆，促进人们修心，思考虚无。这个圆是一笔画成，笔触没有犹豫也不能多做思考，据说可以显示出画圆之人的精神状态：如果一个人思想明澈，没有任何思想或意图，就可以画出一个匀称有力的禅圆。

　　比洛多继续查找其他信息，他了解到，禅圆有很多种解释：它可以代表完美、真相、无穷、简易、四季的交替或是旋转的轮子。总的来说，禅圆象征着圆圈、宇宙的周期性、历史总是在重复、最终总会返回起点。从这个意义上来说，它与希腊的衔尾蛇标志类似。

　　禅圆是一个含义丰富且多样的标志，看到这部手稿的最后一页，就能了解这个标志丰富明确的含义，那一页上的俳句与第一页的俳句是一样的：

> 时光若流水，
> 彷徨复彷徨，
> 恋恋崎岖礁石上。

把开头的诗放在结尾，绝非偶然。格朗普雷是有意这样安排的，他要让他的诗集犹如循环。末尾采用开头的诗，让人想到了禅圆，表示这本书在不断地重复。

比洛多合上手稿，沉浸在思绪中。他真遗憾出版商拒绝了这份手稿。这部作品集结了格朗普雷的最好作品，首首都是上佳之作，现在被人一口拒绝，实在不公平，出版社的人显然都是糊涂蛋。但世界上又不是只有他们一家出版社。比洛多再次上网，找到了魁北克出版诗歌的大出版社，并且做出了决定：他要把手稿投到别的出版社。别的地方肯定会有人欣赏那些诗歌。

他要让这本诗集出版。他感觉这就好像在完成别人的临终托付。他最起码能为格朗普雷做这件事，毕竟是因为格朗普雷，他才能开辟一条通往塞格琳的路。

第十四章

独木舟之上，
硬鳞鱼在空气里，
将窒息而亡。

做一只青蛙，
透过皮肤来呼吸，
是好事一桩。

对瓢虫来说，
雨滴在树叶之上，
如一场天灾。

尽责的主人，
俯身拾起污秽物，
谁才是主子？

拉优西拉德，

清澈碧波如芭蕉，

创作的短歌。

　　比洛多对十七世纪的优秀俳句诗人芭蕉很熟悉，但短歌是什么？他倒是听说过短歌。他记得去年秋天钻研文学的时候曾看过短歌。

　　只消一会儿工夫，他就在格朗普雷收藏的书中找到了相关的书籍。短歌是最古老、最高贵经典的日本诗歌形式，只有皇家宫廷才有这种艺术形式。短歌是俳句的前身，就像是俳句的"古老祖先"。短歌更长，有五行而非三行，由两部分组成：第一部分是由十七个音节组成的三行押韵诗，犹如古老的俳句；第二部分是额外的对句，由两行七个音节的诗句组成，与第一部分呼应，并且带给整首诗全新的方向。比洛多了解到，两个部分都有其特别的主题。俳句属于短诗，传递的是理智，往往还涉及对自然的观察，和俳句不同，短歌则要感情充沛，具有高雅的情趣。短歌创作者致力于探索高贵的主题和感情，比如爱、孤独和死亡。短歌旨在描述复杂的情感。

　　比洛多不由得颤抖起来。塞格琳提到短歌，有什么目的？

是微妙的信息，还是邀请？

短歌是用来表达感情的。这不正是比洛多渴望的吗？有时候，碍于俳句的限制，他不总是束手束脚的吗？老实说，他不是早已厌倦了描绘天气预报、晾衣绳和小鸟这样的主题？现在难道不应该思考更宏大、更美丽的东西，并且打破禁锢他的枷锁？他难道不渴望更进一步，最终袒露自己的心声？

比洛多穿上和服，开始写作，急于尝试这种陌生的形式，并且惊讶地发现他不费吹灰之力就掌握了这种诗歌形式。诗句仿佛自行出现，如同成熟的水果一样掉落在他的手里。

> 有些花仿佛，
> 历时七年方盛开。
> 漫漫时光长，
> 我渴望倾诉衷肠，
> 爱你至地老天荒。

比洛多兴高采烈，很为自己写的第一首短歌骄傲，飞快地到外面把这首诗寄了出去。等到心中的激动平息下来，他才开始思考他都写了什么，脑中疑窦丛生。

认真想一想，给塞格琳寄一首有别于往常的诗歌，真的明智吗？他担心的不是诗歌的形式，而是内容：看到如此直接的告白，如此突然将从前有所保留的情感袒露出来，那个年轻女人会有怎样的反应？会不会让她与自己疏远？他们之间那甜蜜微妙的关系是否会破裂？比洛多是不是太大胆了？

他现在真后悔自己那么性急，但泼出去的水已经收不回来了：那首短歌此刻就在街对面的邮箱底部，拿不回来了。至少从理论上来讲是这样的。罗伯特是不是快到中午时去邮箱收信？

快到中午的时候，比洛多去等罗伯特，他就像个神经兮兮的哨兵，在邮箱周围走来走去，完全没听到从南方北归的候鸟发出的鸣叫声。终于，在半个小时后，面包车出现了。车子停在路边，罗伯特下车，看到他的老朋友比洛多，他高兴地大叫起来。比洛多没有理会罗伯特的热情，直接说是来找罗伯特帮忙的。罗伯特一开始有些犹豫，说比洛多让他做的事很不合规矩，但他很快就不再犹豫，毕竟比起他们之间牢不可破的兄弟情，那些愚蠢的规则又算得了什么。

邮局职员罗伯特把邮箱里的东西取出来，便让比洛多和他一起上车，因为在车上可以避开别人窥探的眼睛，他把袋子里的东西倒出来，让比洛多找出他说他寄错了的那封信。比洛多胡乱说了几句感谢的话，便摊开各种包裹、信封、用过的注射器、偷来的曲棍球衫等从邮箱里取来的脏东西，找到了他的信。现在危险消除了，比洛多如释重负，但他却微微有些失望，连他自己也说不清这是为什么。

罗伯特用那双爱打探的眼睛一直盯着信封上的地址。这位邮局职员一点也不相信比洛多提出的蹩脚借口，猜测比洛多肯定是为了女人才这样，他就问比洛多瓜德罗普岛的塞格琳是什么人，比洛多出自本能地把信藏在夹克里。他是很感激罗伯特，却不愿意谈起这件事，便说这是个秘密。出乎意料的是，罗伯特并没有追问，只是提醒他的朋友，除非等他下班和他一起去喝酒庆祝，否则他绝对不肯善罢甘休。比洛多有些犹豫，他很清楚这样的邀请轻而易举就能让事情失控，但罗伯特帮了他的忙，他又怎么能拒绝他呢?

第十五章

比洛多的梦里出现了笑声。他醒来后，过了一会儿，他才意识到他和衣躺在榻榻米上，百叶窗开着，早晨的阳光洒在他的脸上。他很想起来，但马上放弃了这个念头，他的头跳动着作痛，他只好平躺在榻榻米上。昨夜纵欲的回忆断断续续地出现在他的脑海中。安大略大街上有个酒吧，昨天晚上，他们首先去了那里。一杯杯苏格兰威士忌出现在吧台上。接下来的事情就有些模糊了：他们好像去了斯坦利大街上的一家艳舞俱乐部，他们坐在一个小隔间里，性感的美女在他们边上扭腰摆臀，之后，罗伯特硬拖他去了挂着按摩院牌子的妓院，从妓院出来，他们去了一家明亮的餐馆，坐在长条软凳上吃了夏威夷比萨，这之后呢？他们是去了酒吧，还是去了俱乐部？他对后面的事是一点儿也记不得了。

罗伯特没完没了地问他问题，一次次轻率地打听那封信和塞格琳的事，罗伯特不停地发动攻势，事情越来越失控。这位邮局职员显然是要利用他喝醉的机会，挖出全部内幕。比洛多都吐露了什么？他必须承认他对此一无所知。他都告诉罗伯特什么了？在关于昨晚的记忆胶片上，那些乌漆墨黑的部分都是什么？

他在梦中听到的笑声再次响起，只是比洛多现在是醒着的，而笑声来自隔壁房间。有人在客厅里笑。比洛多惊讶地发现这正是罗伯特的独特笑声，并且意识到，那个邮局职员就在这里，就在相邻的房间里。一段新鲜的记忆朝他涌来：他忽然想起，疯狂了一晚，在凌晨时分，他竟然愚蠢地让他的朋友开车送他回家。而且是这个新家！这个他的秘密避难所！

他想起罗伯特喝得醉醺醺的，惊奇地发现他竟然谁也没告诉就鬼鬼祟祟搬了家，而且惊讶于比洛多的新居竟然是日式装潢。他想到他的朋友在屋里到处转，寻找艺伎，喝光了一瓶清酒，在浴缸里撒尿，撞翻了一个小茶几，最后瘫倒在榻榻米上睡着了，发出的呼噜声大得就像是一架 B-52 轰炸机在城市上方准备投放原子弹。比洛多的偏头痛又开始了。他犯了不可饶恕的错误！现在，他的私人堡垒再也不是什么秘密了。罗伯特知道了。他就在客厅，他在笑。到底是什么这么好笑？

比洛多强忍着恶心感，从榻榻米上起来，走进走廊。罗伯特又笑了。比洛多扶着墙壁，来到客厅门口，他看到罗伯特穿着四角裤和汗衫坐在书桌边的扶手椅上。他在看他显然觉得很搞笑的东西，而那个东西正是塞格琳写的俳句。

抽屉打开着。那个年轻女人的诗歌散落在书桌上，罗伯特拿着几首诗，目光落在诗句上，完全是一种亵渎，边看还边抓挠生殖器，甚至还好意思用他那低沉沙哑类似猿人的声音朗读着。

"'它们勇敢地，炫耀雪崩的外衣，心却很柔弱。'"罗伯特大笑着说，"什么叫'雪崩的外衣'？那照这样说，口活不叫吹箫，该叫吹雪了。"

看到罗伯特穿着内衣，用令人恶心的肥胖手指捏着塞格琳的精妙诗歌，用他那阴森森的目光和沙哑的笑声玷污着它们，比洛多感觉自己血管里的血都变成了冰。他用冷淡机械的声音命令罗伯特把信纸还给他，但罗伯特似乎没把他的话放在心上。

"等等。"他翻着诗歌说，"别的诗更差劲。"

罗伯特故技重施，用可笑的假声又朗读了一首诗。比洛多向他走去。罗伯特早就料到了这一点。他一跃从椅子上起来，跑向房间的另一端。比洛多在后面追他，决定不惜一切代价也要把珍贵的诗稿夺回来。他最终识破了这个可怜小丑的花招，一把把他抓住，但那个白痴说什么也不肯放手，结果，不可避免的结局发生了……比洛多不知所措地盯着依旧被罗伯特握在手里的碎纸，然后看看他自己手里的纸片。

"老天！"罗伯特哈哈笑着说。

"滚出去。"比洛多冷冰冰地命令道。

"放松。"罗伯特挑衅地喊道，"别动气啊，不就是几首破诗吗，不值得！"

他真的说了"破诗"？他的血刚才瞬间凝固，现在又立即融解，达到了沸点。他猛地击出一拳，揍在了罗伯特的鼻子上。罗伯特一下子撞破了樱花树图案的折叠屏风，朝下猛撞在屏风后面的矮桌上。比洛多从他的手指间把诗稿碎片抓了过来。罗伯特被打得头昏眼花，捂着流血的鼻子，他摇摇晃晃地站起来，还有胆子把事情搞大。他骂骂咧咧，挥动手臂，试图反击，但他的拳头只是扫到了比洛多的耳朵。比洛多猛打在他的肚子上，算是回敬。罗伯特一下子泄了气，他被打得喘不过气，再也提不起勇气去攻击。比洛多趁机揪着他的马甲把他提起来，拖着他向走廊走去，刚打开门，就把他丢了出去。罗伯特一下子摔倒在台阶上，仰面向下滑了3级。比洛多把他的衣服扔在他身上，插上插销。

他简直不敢相信。他一直都是个连蚂蚁都舍不得杀死的人，但就在刚才，他竟然打了他最好的朋友。不，应该说是他从前的朋友。但他眼下有一件更迫切的事情要担心。现在是危机时刻：塞格琳的几首最好的俳句都被撕碎了。比洛多权当没听到罗伯特在门外大声咒骂，发出可怕的警告，他对罗伯特的大力砸门声置若罔闻，只是拿出一卷透明胶带，将珍贵的信纸贴合在一起。罗伯特开始在门外威胁，说什么他不会就此罢休，迟早会回来算账，但比洛多什么都没听见，只是全神贯注地像在进行外科手术一样，修补着残缺不全的诗稿。

过了很长时间，罗伯特的喊叫声消失了，塞格琳的诗作也都修补好了。比洛多明明记得他把那封没有寄出的信塞进了夹克口袋，他伸手去找，才发现信不见了——那封信和里面的短歌都不见了。

他不记得信到哪里去了，是他在昨晚寻欢作乐时犯了傻，把信弄丢了，还是卑鄙的罗伯特把信偷走了？

第十六章

比洛多走进玛德琳诺餐厅吃午饭，他注意到罗伯特和他在邮局的同事坐在老位子上。一眼就能看到他的鼻子都肿了，青一块紫一块的。比洛多感觉人们充满敌意的目光落在他身上，罗伯特肯定添油加醋地讲了他们打架的事儿。比洛多试着不去理会别人的敌意。他坐在柜台边上。塔尼娅走过来，把一碗汤放在他面前，他用勺子搅拌汤，思考着一件棘手的事：怎么做才能把被偷走的短歌拿回来。诗真的在罗伯特那里吗？显然不可以直接过去问他，尤其是现在还有别人在场。

他心想，怎么才能想出一个两全其美的办法，既让自己不妥协，又让罗伯特不拿这件事大做文章？怎么才能把信拿回来，既不用受辱也不用道歉，更加用不着看那家伙的脸色？比洛多心不在焉地嚼着肉馅土豆馅饼，盼着罗伯特能主动走过来，说出一个把信赎回去的数目，但这样的事儿自然不会发生，看那个家伙的态度，就知道他会恨自己一辈子。

吃完午饭，他走出洗手间，差一点和塔尼娅撞在了一起，她就站在门边等他。这个年轻的女人笑着说是来感谢他的。当然是为了那首诗。比洛多看到她拿着一张纸。是那首短歌！

塔尼娅的眼中闪烁着幸福的泪水，她说她在柜台上发现这首诗就在他的账单和现金的边上，真是又惊又喜。她承认她被这首诗深深地感动了，然后，她低下头，红着脸，说她也有相同的感觉。比洛多目瞪口呆，终于恍然大悟：她以为他按照承诺，写了那首短歌给她，她还以为……真是太可怕了，他都喘不上气了。他连一句整话都说不出来，更没有办法消除塔尼娅的误解，他现在能做的就是站在那里傻笑。那个姑娘肯定把他的迷惑当成了害羞，老练地不再提起这个话题，只是用亮晶晶的眼睛看了他一眼，便回去工作了。

比洛多终于缓过神来。眼前的情况给了他一个措手不及，他有些发蒙。他一眼就看到邪恶阴谋的实施者就坐在餐馆的另一端，罗伯特的脸上挂着邪恶的微笑，足以解释一切。那个浑蛋竟然幸灾乐祸地看着他的复仇！比洛多抓起夹克，悄悄离开餐馆，但见到塔尼娅羞怯地冲他轻轻挥手，他还是回应了一下。他义愤填膺，便去罗伯特的面包车边等他。

十分钟后，罗伯特走了过来，脸上依然挂着他特有的笑，得意扬扬的样子十分可憎，他问比洛多什么时候结婚。比洛多怒不可遏，责备他使用下三烂的手段，把塔尼娅牵扯到他们两个人的恩怨中。罗伯特冷嘲热讽，说什么自己只是想让塔尼娅开心，但不太明白她为什么对比洛多这样一个愚蠢的浑蛋这么热情。是呀，比洛多觉得自己确实傻，不然早就应该看出罗伯特是这么一个浑蛋。罗伯特反驳道，浑蛋也比傻瓜强，并且警告比洛多，现在只是给他点颜色瞧瞧，自那以后，他们之间就算开战了。罗伯特说完这话就快步离开了。

比洛多很了解罗伯特这个人，知道他有多凶狠残暴，那天剩下的时间，比洛多一直担心罗伯特会使出折磨人的招数整治自己，罗伯特的威胁迫在眉睫。可以肯定的是，自己的确尊重塔尼娅，不管她到时候有多失望，他都必须把真相告诉她。

没过多久，罗伯特就动手了。第二天，比洛多来到分理处，一眼就看到员工休息室的布告牌上贴着一份他那首短歌的复印件，上面还带有罗伯特伪造的签名，他不由得惊慌失措，复印纸是粉色的，这样更有视觉冲击力。还有很多复印件被发到了整个邮局，特别是分理处，从那里不断有笑声传来。好像全世界都看了他写的那首诗。结果那天人们都拿这件事开玩笑：人们一碰到比洛多，就会送给他一些暗示着爱情的花花草草。邮差比洛多无计可施，只好默不作声，坚强地忍受着大家的冷落。

他终于熬到了出去送邮件的时候，不由得感觉如释重负，但在外面快步走上三个钟头只能勉强舒缓他的神经。

快到中午，比洛多向玛德琳诺餐厅走去，他打定主意要和塔尼娅谈谈，把真相向她和盘托出，但当他走进餐馆，他意识到罗伯特的诡计再次得逞了，他来晚了一步：人们连看都不看他一眼，在他经过的时候，说话声戛然而止，但在邮递员的老座位上，大家都围在罗伯特身边，嘲笑比洛多，罗伯特的眼里闪烁着恶毒的目光，而且鼻子现在是紫色的。塔尼娅看到他，表现得好像根本不认识他，走进厨房不见了人影儿。

"塞格琳！塞格琳！"那帮小丑在餐馆另一端疲倦地大呼小叫。

比洛多的脸色变得煞白。这个时候，他情愿用一切来交换大家接纳他。他转身刚要走，却想起他必须先去和塔尼娅谈谈，便勇敢地走进餐厅。他忍受着别人的大呼小叫、含沙射影，走到柜台边坐下。

"塞格琳！让我登上你那通往瓜德罗普岛的单桅帆船吧！"

比洛多攥紧拳头，不确定他还能忍多久。塔尼娅端着一托盘食物走出厨房。他冲她比画了一下，但她完全无视他，反而去给那群邮局的职员上菜了。那些人自然不会放过这个大好机

孤 独 邮 差

会，问她是否打算今年去瓜德罗普岛度假，还说要是她不嫉妒
她的情敌，完全可以来段三角恋，并且一指，说什么她的未婚
夫"力比多"正在柜台那里等着她，要是她快点，说不定还
能得到一首专门写给她的情诗。

　　她一言不发地给他们上了菜，一看就知道很生气。最后，
她觉得看起来好像是她让比洛多更加煎熬了，于是就站在柜台
的另一边让他点菜，只是她态度冷淡，活像一座冰山，就算来
十几艘泰坦尼克号，也能撞沉了。她问他要点什么，鸭肉？像
她一样的动不动就被骗的傻鸭子？还是要美味的鹅肉？要不就
来点试验新诗的豚鼠？比洛多表达了深刻的歉意，解释说她完
全误会了，他必须和她私下里谈谈，但塔尼娅说谈不谈已经没
意义了，根本没什么好说的，她把一个纸团扔到柜台上。

　　"比洛多，把你的诗还给你！"她厉声道。

　　邮局职员落座的角落爆发出一阵掌声，餐馆里的其他人也
鼓起掌来，塔尼娅有了很多支持者——所有来吃午饭的人都饶
有兴味地关注着事情的进展。比洛多跟着塔尼娅走到厨房门边，
低声发誓这并不是他的错，那首诗本不是写给她的，而且也不
应该送给她，但塔尼娅并不相信，质问他为什么昨天不说清楚，
而是把她当成了傻瓜。比洛多含含糊糊地解释着，但她打断了

他，说她再也不想听到他那些恶心的小把戏，让他和罗伯特去找别的受害者，离她远点儿。又是一阵掌声响起，算是对她这鼓舞人心的命令表示支持。

塔尼娅的眼泪夺眶而出，她跑进厨房，餐馆的厨师马丁内斯站在厨房门口，这个人足有两百多斤，手里还拿着把菜刀。比洛多没有选择，只好退出去，他快步离开餐馆，活像是被驱逐出来的一样。他很想尽快逃到天涯海角，但马路在他的脚下摇晃，他的腿不听使唤，一屁股坐在台阶上，免得摔倒在地。

他在台阶上整整坐了五分钟，努力克服无助的感觉，盼着能压下在他的肚子里不断翻腾的羞愧和愤怒。这时候，那些邮局职员从餐馆里走了出来，罗伯特走在最前面。罗伯特从他身边走过，显然很享受比洛多那副沮丧的样子，他在一群部下的簇拥下得意扬扬地往前走，他们还唱起了描述瓜德罗普岛异域美景的赞歌。比洛多感觉十分虚弱，根本无力抵抗，他垂下头，坐在那里盯着依然被他握在手里的纸团……

他把纸抚平，仔细一看，这才发现那其实不是原件，也是复印件！比洛多受了刺激，叫住已经走出一百米的罗伯特和他的帮凶。罗伯特停下来，等着比洛多向他跑过去。现在，再也没必要束手束脚了，比洛多要罗伯特把信还给他。罗伯特被这个要求逗乐了，说自己根本就没留着那首低劣的诗，早把它寄出去了，然后，就和同事们一起走了。比洛多愕然地站在原地，听到那首短歌被寄了出去，瞬间就愣住了。

　　经过了这么多折磨，他竟然回到了起点——像是经历了一个轮回。

第十七章

　　那首短歌已经寄给了塞格琳，泼出去的水再也收不回来了，其他的担心都被一扫而空。罗伯特的阴谋诡计、塔尼娅的伤心、邮局、生活和死亡，这些对比洛多而言都不再重要。她收到诗了吗？她看过了吗？她有没有觉得惊讶？她是觉得无聊、失望，还是不屑一顾？说不定正好相反呢——她感动了，满心欢喜，一切都很完美吗？比洛多喜欢第二种假设，塔尼娅最初看到那首诗后的反应增强了他的信心——塞格琳肯定也会有类似的反应，对吧？然后，他忽然想到了罗伯特对那首诗的评价，一下子灰心丧气起来。罗伯特骂他的诗"低劣"。这次会不会让他侥幸给说中了？比洛多为了这件事做了噩梦。在梦中，他看到巨大的嘴唇张张合合，轻蔑地重复着"低劣"这个词。

　　那张嘴属于塞格琳，红色嘴唇，白森森的牙齿，看起来怪吓人的，一直在重复那个残忍的词——低劣。

　　每次都像是有把匕首扎他的心，因为他知道这是事实，他的诗的确低劣，她一次次地这么说来惩罚他的愚蠢，绝对是正确的。塞格琳的牙齿把短歌咬成了无数的碎片，碎片飞往各个方向，散落在最远处的冰冷虚无中。比洛多能在那些碎纸上看到他自己的脸，仿佛那是很多小镜子，他痛苦到了极点……

这就是他的梦境，等他醒来，心里就像敲起了小鼓，整天提心吊胆，担惊受怕。他开始思考，是不是不应该坐以待毙，而是应该采取预防措施，是不是应该写信给塞格琳坦白一切，让她知道格朗普雷已经去世了，他自己只是个可怜的冒充者。

这样的话，他的良心至少能好过一点，但他改变了主意，让自己理智点，他很清楚不可能这样坦白，不然的话，他所做的一切就将大白于天下，为这段给他的生活带来无穷乐趣的通信敲响丧钟。

比洛多就像个风向标一样在希望和放弃之间来回摆动，也恰好印证了一句话：当你拿不准结果的时候，最煎熬的莫过于等待了。

塞格琳终于回信了。比洛多快步走出他工作的小隔间，走进男厕。他屏住呼吸，准备迎接他的胆大妄为带来的后果，他打开信纸。

纸上有一首五行诗。她用一首短歌作为答复：

闷热的雾夜，

潮湿床单轻柔地，

裹着腿和臀，

为寻你迷失自己，

我是盛放的花朵。

　　比洛多眨眨眼，还以为他看错了，但那上面写得明明白白。
不会有错。那些字是真的，清清楚楚，她的确写了那首诗。

　　他原以为塞格琳会写信拒绝他，或者写一首他们常写的简
单俳句，或者至多写一首像他那样的浪漫短歌，但他做梦也没
想到她会写这么一首充满肉欲和热情的诗。她到底是怎么想的？
比洛多感觉到他的下体一阵激动，这才意识到他竟然勃起了，
这样惊人的生理反应让他惊慌不已。塞格琳的信从未引起过这
样的反应。这倒不是说这是他第一次因为她有生理反应，每次
他梦到她，他都会这样。但现在是在光天化日之下，而他还是
清醒的，怎么会这样？

　　显然是因为这首短歌中包含异乎寻常的内容，具有明显的
色情特征。他真希望知道，塞格琳在写诗时是否预料到了这样
的结果。她是无意的，还是有心的？比洛多应该如何回应？对

于这样一首诗，他该作何回应？

　　夜里，他梦到一条蛇在蕨类植物中蜿蜒爬行，鬼鬼祟祟地爬过光滑的棕色树根，那棵树的树干长满了藤本植物。只是那棵树不是树，而是一个人的身体，是塞格琳的赤裸身体，旁边是她的长笛。为了不吵醒她，那条蛇悄悄地爬到她的喉咙上，缠住她的四肢，从她的双乳之间爬到她的肚子上，吐着分叉的舌头品味着空气中的气味，然后，它继续向下，爬向那个幽暗的深谷，爬向她双腿之间毛发浓密的三角地带……比洛多因为这个蛇梦如痴如醉，醒来之后兴奋不已，但相比前一天，他现在的状态还算正常：他的阴茎一直是勃起的，他的感觉是那么急切，只有当他把塞格琳的事赶出脑海的片刻，才有所缓解。

　　他在重读那首诗的时候，不禁怀疑他是不是会错意了，他觉得诗中含有色情的暗示，但那是否只是他邪恶的想象，但他认为不是。那首短歌的确充满肉欲。不管塞格琳是有意为之，还是无意之举，只有一种回复她的方式：

　　　　　　　　你不仅是花，

　　　　　　　　你是芳香的花园，

我为你疯狂，

我进入你的花冠，

轻啜着你的花蜜。

第十八章

海浪冲沙滩，
荡来一个咸的吻，
唇齿的相交，
在分分合合之间，
终于紧锁在一起。

复活节巧克力蛋，
黄色的彩带，
我渴望轻咬，
从赤裸肩头滑落，
你的裙吊带。

你若要咬我，
轻点，食人怪。
将我整个儿吞下，

不然下一个，是你，

被我一口吞下去。

我将成为风，

吹乱你一头秀发，

偷迷人香气，

我滑到你的裙下，

让你的皮肤燃烧。

我脚趾蠕动，

不住地卷曲弯动，

因为快乐而兴奋，

因我的手指，

我对你思念至深。

这是甜蜜的陶醉，是撩人的狂热，让你过着双倍紧张刺激的生活，这就像是你无意抵抗的湍流，你只会屈服，再说了，这正是比洛多希望的。他唯一的野心便是继续这种充满肉欲的冒险，胆大详细地描写身体，尽情地体验狂喜。这份追求占满

了他的心。他很少踏出房门，对五月的美景视而不见，即便这
是他最喜爱的月份。他没有再去玛德琳诺餐厅，他觉得塔尼娅
八成会认为他是要嘲笑她，所以他不敢再次露面。事实上，他
也不去上班了。他在分理处受尽了屈辱，再也承受不了，于是
他提出休六个月的无薪假期。现在他的时间都是他自己的，他
把他的全部献给了塞格琳。

乳房在天边，
如同圆润的沙丘，
我渴望品尝，
用你的甜蜜安抚，
渴望爱的吸血鬼。

我迷失沙漠，
嘴唇渴望地爬行，
绿洲终出现，
我伸出舌尖，
深插入你的肚脐。

你那双美腿，
反射着洁白月光，
雕塑家用那，
上好红木来雕刻，
你纤细光滑的腿。

你将我举起，
我弯曲拥抱自己，
塑造，焚烧我，
你的双手摆弄我，
你的小玩物。

裙子掩盖下，
你双腿的交汇处，
藏着一条河，
啊，神秘的亚马逊，
让我逆流而上吧。

孤 独 邮 差

> 你的衣服，从
> 我的衣服上滑过，
> 若是可以，将
> 它们缝合在一起，
> 能触碰每寸肌肤。

短歌真的是表达欲望的最佳工具吗？比洛多曾经很喜欢用这种诗歌形式来表达感情，但现在却觉得十分沉重，似乎太伤脑筋。他希望找到一种更为轻松的办法，便决定回归简单基本的俳句，他感觉这种诗歌形式更有助于表达他心中无尽的欲望。

> 高耸的双乳，
> 如同傲人的山峰，
> 就在我手下。

塞格琳肯定很赞成他主动改换诗歌形式，不然也不会立即回复了一首俳句：

强健的根基，

　　在手中悸动，

炙热的体液奔涌。

　　他们就这样继续用俳句通信：去掉了多余的词汇，就好像
把衣服都脱在通往卧室的路上，只剩下诗歌的精华。但比洛多
并不满意，他再也受不了缓慢的平邮，于是开始使用快递。塞
格琳也如法炮制——这样一来，他们的等待周期就缩短了。他
们的通信频率加快，平稳的呼吸变成了气喘吁吁，然而，这对
比洛多而言还是不够快，他开始不再等回复就给瓜德罗普岛的
那个女人寄信，很快，他就每天给她寄一首俳句。塞格琳也开
始不等回复，就给他寄俳句。几乎每天早晨都有来自她的信放
在他家的门垫上。他们互寄诗歌，速度快，充满激情，虽然不
用遵循一定的时间顺序，却以一种奇怪的方式互相呼应：

　　　胴体如鲜花，

　　在娇嫩的花瓣中，

暗藏着珍珠。

孤 独 邮 差

你长驱直入，
用你的身体，冲击，
我那温热的身体。

我向你移动，
你让我长驱直入，
用嘴吞没我。

在我的身体，
看过每一道风景。
在我的湖泊畅游。

我游走在你，
那核心地带，
是你首府的中心。

海啸大爆发，
我的心猛烈爆炸，
超新星升起。

猛烈的海啸，
岩浆剧烈地迸发，
我长眠于此。

我随波逐流，
我只是一种色彩，
忘记了姓名。

风帆如繁星，
太阳风猛地吹起，
直到天尽头。

第十九章

　　人不可能永远待在云端。地球重力终于还是将比洛多拉回到地上，诗歌给他带来的缓慢但强烈的亢奋感依然让他震撼不已。爱情确实可以让人生出翅膀。他从未像现在这样隔空拥抱一个女人。

　　他感觉塞格琳距离他那么近，他感觉她属于他，她就在他的身体里，他也在她的身体里，他知道，她也经历了一场内心的爆炸。他很肯定他们两个同时达到了高潮。在那之后，还能写些什么呢？这样的激情澎湃过后，写出怎样的诗歌，才不会叫人失望？是在爱人的耳畔喁喁细语，送她进入梦乡？

　　比洛多苦苦思索着，他穿上和服，闷闷不乐地看了一眼窗外，只见雪花懒洋洋地落在山毛榉大街上。已经是冬天了？已经过了这么久？难道他对外界竟然无视到了这种程度，所以夏天犹如流星一闪而过，他却只关注自己的一片小天地，没注意到？然后他仔细一看，才发现那不是雪，而是被风从附近公园的树上吹来的花粉。猛一看，花粉和雪花真的是一模一样。蕴含在夏天里的冬天。这样的超自然景观很符合比洛多的心境，带给他写诗的灵感：

羽绒覆沥青，

如五彩纸屑骤下，

第一场大雪，

轻柔懒散地落在，

夜晚爱欲的躯体。

以云为伪装——

月亮变成新模样，

月光柔如水，

此刻泼洒于游廊，

你是我唯一思念。

干燥的峡谷，

河溪早已变枯竭，

寸草不生地，

似我的寂寞灵魂，

殷殷期盼你的信。

孤 独 邮 差

日日复夜夜，
无论我身在何处，
你常伴着我，
是你写来的诗歌，
让我告别了孤单。

狗儿在守卫，
它睡觉的软垫子，
她愿为它死，
女士请让我，
当你傻傻的骑士。

我心花怒放，
是你卑微的仆人，
若得你青睐，
我还可以做你那，
梦中的情人。

我无惧风车，

凶猛巨人 ①又何妨

我只惧怕你，

看到我忧伤面容，

是那般难过。

学校的墙上，

古老钟表忠实地，

将准确时间，

展示给街坊四邻，

我心只为你跳动。

　　比洛多无意中看了一眼日历，惊讶地发现八月就快过去了。格朗普雷离开这个世界就快一年了。比洛多的生活发生巨变的那个重要纪念日很快就到了，但随着日子一天天临近，他并不觉得恐惧或是悲伤。因为，相比死亡，出生更值得纪念，他自己的重生更值得纪念，他与塞格琳之间的美好通信更值得纪念。显而易见，那个日子只对他一个人重要，在她的眼中，那不过

----

① 堂吉诃德曾将风车当成了巨人。

孤 独 邮 差

是个普普通通的日子，但即便如此，这个幸福纪念日的到来还
是值得庆祝，只是他要谨慎一点：

> 阴冷的冬日，
>
> 你的诗似我的春，
>
> 爱却如夏日，
>
> 褐色、金色的秋天，
>
> 储备了什么？

几天后，塞格琳的回复到了，却让他陷入了无边的恐惧中。
塞格琳也对这个秋天抱着很高的希望……

> 我儿时梦想，
>
> 去看加拿大的秋，
>
> 我买了车票，
>
> 将于二十日抵达，
>
> 你能否与我相会？

第二十章

　　甜美喜悦的爱情瞬间化为了一场噩梦。她怎么会有这么疯狂的念头？来观赏加拿大的秋天？她为什么这么做？

　　绝对不可能。塞格琳不可能就这样出现在蒙特利尔，不然就完了，一切都将轰然毁灭。她知道格朗普雷的样貌，他们曾经交换过那些该死的照片，这样一来，他怎么才能继续隐瞒她？但他怎么才能劝说她放弃这段疯狂的旅程？他怎么才能拒绝她？

　　她将在九月二十日抵达，也就是说，比洛多有三个礼拜去找出合适的答案，去编造借口。或许他可以写信告诉她，他自己也要出门旅行，整个九月都不在国内，遗憾不能接待她。但要是她提议延后行程，等他回来后再来呢？

　　她怎么这么愚蠢？她难道就没想到，她将毁掉一切，将让他们在眼下保持的完美关系陷入危机？但这自然不是她的错：她根本不可能知道的。比洛多不得不承认，会出现这样的不幸，全都是他的责任。他早就该料到迟早会发生这种事，他怎么能

孤 独 邮 差

如此盲目呢?

现在该怎么办?说他最近做了整容手术,长相和以前完全不一样?还是逃跑?搬出这栋她知道地址的公寓,不然到时候她来了之后,肯定会找上门来?对于他的失踪这个令人费解的谜团,她爱怎么猜测,就怎么猜测好了。但在那之后,他要怎么面对内心的愧疚、懦弱和破灭的希望?他要怎么忘记?怎么活下去?

根本没有可行的办法。比洛多知道他到了山穷水尽的地步,就像一只无辜的老鼠被残忍的钢铁捕鼠夹夹住了。现在,宁静的美梦结束了,供他飘浮许久的快乐气泡破碎了,这样的毁灭让他的心里充满了无助的愤怒。他无法让自己接受失去她,却也提不起勇气面对她。所有的选择都是可怕的,所有的门都关闭了。他走进了死胡同。

第二天天刚亮,电话就响了。比洛多没心思接电话,便任由客厅里的答录机接听电话。有人留了口信,是一个出版商,他曾把《禅圆》的手稿寄给了许多出版商,打电话来的就是其中一个。那个人简要地说他很喜欢那本诗集,要将其出版,请作者马上回复。比洛多原本蜷缩成胎儿的姿势躺着,听到录音,他马上起来，又把录音听了一遍。

命运有时候会送来怪异至极的转折点。他如果在一天前收到这个消息，一定满心雀跃，现在他只觉得是在受折磨。这又有什么用呢？

格朗普雷的诗集出版了，又不能化解他现在所处的困境，只会雪上加霜。一切都完了。

他拿起手稿，随意翻看着，就像是从塔罗牌中寻找天机，他看到了这样一首俳句：

冲破地平线，

往天地尽头眺望，

来迎接死亡。

这首诗填满了他的心，忽然带来了全新的意义，比洛多突然想到了一个主意——这是唯一能解决他所有问题的办法。

他直起身体。他知道该怎么办了。

第二十一章

这条路是明摆着的。他必须使用这个办法，但必须事先筹措一番。比洛多给打电话来的出版商写了一封信，同意让他如愿出版《禅圆》。他把信放在书桌上显眼的地方，又给金鱼比尔喂了双倍它最喜欢的鱼食，算是和金鱼道别，感谢它坚贞不渝的友谊。他准备好离开了。

装饰客厅天花板的巨大镂空横梁正好可以派上用场。他把叶片形状的小桌推到横梁正下方，然后摘掉和服的腰带，试试它够不够结实。他很满意，不由得想到了童年时光，当时，他是一名童子军，过着无忧无虑的日子。他随手就打了一个活结。他希望能走得干净一些。他可不愿意割腕或是饮弹自尽，毕竟这两种办法都太叫人恶心。比洛多希望能够有尊严地离开这个世界，留下的痕迹越少越好——上吊无疑是将混乱降到最低的办法。

他爬上小桌，将腰带一端系在房梁上，然后把活结绕在脖子上。他准备好了。现在是时候拥抱死亡了。他只要用脚后跟把桌子踢翻，他的痛苦就结束了。比洛多做了个深呼吸，闭上眼，然后……

门铃划破了宁静。

比洛多吓了一大跳，不确定该怎么做。他决定等一会儿，盼着闯入者会自行离开，不再按门铃，但门铃再次响起。他既松了口气，又觉得恼火，这两种感情混合在一起，是那么奇怪。真是的！谁这么大胆子，竟然敢在这么关键的时刻打搅他，毕竟他已经有几个月没有访客了。他把活结拿开，从桌上走下来，走到门边，从窥测孔向外张望。门外有一张扭曲的脸，是塔尼娅。

居然是塔尼娅。他都快把这个人忘了。如果比洛多还欠这世上哪个人一个解释，那无疑就是这位年轻的女招待了。他隐隐有些害怕，但还是打开了三道锁和四条安全锁链，把门打开。塔尼娅看了一眼站在门口的比洛多，她似乎比他还要惊讶。她焦虑地注视着他，问他是否还好，说她觉得他变了很多。比洛多听了这些话，并不觉得惊讶：受到了这么多折磨，现在又决定拥抱死亡，他肯定就跟个活死人差不多了。他露出淡淡的微笑，并且告诉她，他现在感觉好极了。那个女孩显然不信，她为自己打扰到他道了歉，并且前言不搭后语地解释一番，说是从罗伯特那里得到了他的地址。比洛多也想为上次在餐厅里发生的事道歉，但她抢先开口，说大部分责任都在她：塔尼娅去找罗伯特理论，了解了实情，得知整件事和比洛多没关系，此外，她说如果不是她自作多情，也不会发生那么多事，不是吗？

她紧张地倒换双脚，一看就知道很尴尬，像是在等他确定她刚才说的属实，或是推翻她所说的一切。看到他没有反应，她便道出了此行的目的，说她将离开此地，她已经辞掉了餐馆的工作，准备搬到郊区。

她是否期待他做出特别的反应？他这样无动于衷，是否让她失望了？即便是这样，她也没有表露出来，而是交给他一张纸，说是上面写着她的新地址，以防他可以……要是他乐意的话……比洛多看了看那张纸，他注意到她小心地用日式毛笔字写了她的新地址和电话号码。她写的字很好看，他热情地赞美了她几句。她请他在方便的时候和她联系。他承诺一定会。她又叫他不要有任何勉强，说完强挤出一丝笑容。接下来他们沉默了一会儿，气氛有些尴尬。他们就这样站在楼梯平台上，一言不发，都不敢看对方，这么过了看似漫无止境的十秒钟。最后，塔尼娅打破沉默，说她该走了。她道了别，僵硬地走下台阶。

她来到人行道上，扭过头看到他仍在那里，然后，她加快脚步，匆匆离开。比洛多好像看到她的脸上有什么东西在闪耀。

是眼泪吗？他目送她离开，一股强烈的感情攫取了他。就好像他的心里出现了一个令人痛苦的空洞，好像一个美好的想法尚未实现就流产了，尚未有机会成形就消失了。好像有一个尖锐的硬块卡在比洛多的喉咙里，他注意到泪水摩挲了他的眼睛。他忽然很想叫住塔尼娅，在她走远前把她喊回来，他举起手，向她伸去，他很想大喊，却发不出任何声音。塔尼娅走到街角右转，消失在了视线中。比洛多的手垂了下去。

街上起风了，将报纸碎片搅起，呈旋涡状飘浮着。比洛多抬头仰望天空，只见天空阴沉，乌云盖顶。一场暴风雨即将来临。他打了个寒战，走进屋内。

比洛多忧伤地关上门，端详着写有塔尼娅新地址和电话号码的纸，他被漂亮的书法迷住了，但塔尼娅带来的全新可能性同样让他着迷。文字和数字像是在那张纸的表面飘浮着，在目光下闪动着光辉。塔尼娅意外来访带来的巨大改变让比洛多困惑不已，那个年轻女人的泪水在他心中搅动起了强烈的感情，一个疯狂的希望突然从她留下的那张纸中涌现出来。

他很想知道他是否忽视了一些极为重要的东西，说不定除了他想到的那些办法，还有其他解决方案？而这个办法更好，能将他带离现在的绝境。人在死后还有来世吗？或者说，他可以选择继续活下去吗？

他走进客厅，不由得愣住了，他发现自己竟然又走到了从天花板悬垂下来的活扣前面。他感觉胃里一阵翻腾。片刻之前，他还觉得死是解脱，现在却发现死亡是那么可怕，一想到他刚才做的事，他直恶心。他忽然感觉非常反胃，赶紧跑进厕所。

等他终于站直身体，他感觉筋疲力尽，只能扶着水槽，这才没有瘫倒在地。他必须提起精神。他把冷水泼到脸上，终于感觉好多了。他甩了甩头，悲伤地看着镜子，只想看看他自己现在是不是和活死人一样。

他被自己的样子吓得魂飞魄散。他从镜中竟然看到了一张胡子拉碴、头发蓬乱的脸，而那张脸与加斯顿·格朗普雷的样貌别无二致。

第 二 十 二 章

　　比洛多难以置信地盯着镜子里本不可能出现的脸，他应该看到他自己的脸，毕竟格朗普雷已经死了。他使劲儿眨眼，希望看到的影像消失，他还拍了自己的脑袋一下，但格朗普雷依然在镜子里，模仿他的每一个动作，带着与他相同的惊愕表情看着他。比洛多觉得他八成是发疯了。过了一会儿，镜中人的一些面部特征吸引了他的注意，让他重新考虑刚才得出的结论是否太过仓促。那张脸并不太像格朗普雷。绿色的眼睛属于比洛多，而故去的格朗普雷有一双蓝眼，眉毛也是一样，他的眉毛不如格朗普雷的浓，他的鼻子小一些，下嘴唇要薄很多。他渐渐地从另一个人的脸中看到了他自己的特征，他承认他不是在做梦，也没有发疯，而镜中人真的是他自己，只不过是出现了一些令人难以置信的变化而已。

　　他很努力寻找合理的解释，他很清楚，这几个月以来，他不注重个人卫生，这才会在镜中看到自己变成了这副模样。他深深地沉浸在诗歌探险中，完全忘记了还要照顾他自己，忽视了最基本的身体护理，甚至都没照过镜子，最后就变成现在这样。

他看到自己颓废的样子，竟然被吓了一大跳。然而，比洛多很想知道，仅仅是因为这样，他才与格朗普雷这么相像吗？难道不是因为他在潜意识里希望能变成格朗普雷？比洛多太希望能变成格朗普雷，结果真的变得一模一样。不管怎么样，效果都是惊人的：几个月没刮胡子，头发凌乱，又穿着格朗普雷的和服，这就使他像极了那个故去之人。难怪塔尼娅看到他现在的样子会这么惊讶——她肯定在一瞬间以为看到了格朗普雷的鬼魂。

比洛多决定马上把脸上的胡子刮掉，他放了热水，拿出剃须刀，却猛地停住了。他忽然想到了一件事：塔尼娅和格朗普雷很熟，却还是认错了，比洛多自己也有片刻的恍惚，那么，一个只看过格朗普雷照片的人，又怎么能认得出来呢？

像是已经变成另一个人的比洛多放下了剃须刀。秋天的约会忽然有了可能，不是吗？

为什么不抓住这个独一无二的机会，欢迎塞格琳到这里来？他既渴望与她用文字沟通，也盼望和她进行面对面的交流，不是吗？他渴望在梦境以外爱她，即便是以格朗普雷的身份去爱她，他要给她一份她值得的爱，他们都值得的爱，到最后，让他们两个可以真正地在一起。

他可以放弃这个扭转命运的良机吗？他有这个权利吗？

那他为什么还要犹豫？还有什么能阻止他邀请她来赏秋，在他的陪伴下，来看一看她梦寐以求的加拿大盛世秋景？

快飞往秋日，

它的等待只为你，

展优美景色。

比洛多沉浸在幸福中，已经开始想象他前往机场，去接那个来自瓜德罗普岛的女人，想象她羞怯地出现在到达口，他和她一起观赏如明信片风景一样的秋日美景，他们的头发在风中飘扬。他似乎品尝到了他们的初吻，期待他们的第一次热烈拥抱，清晨迷失在塞格琳铺散在枕头上的秀发中。但为了让这些美妙的想象成为现实，他必须先把俳句寄出去。

比洛多在信封上贴上邮票，这时，外面的天空中响起了隆隆雷声。打雷了。一整个上午天都阴沉沉的，暴风雨终于如约而至，豆大的雨点噼里啪啦砸在客厅的玻璃窗上。

比洛多绝不会让恶劣的天气阻止他把诗歌寄出去，于是他拿起雨伞，走了出去。他站在楼梯平台上，一道闪电照亮了街道，紧跟着是一道响亮的炸雷声，雨势忽然转大。在街道的

孤 独 邮 差

另一边，透过瓢泼大雨，他看到了一辆邮车。到收信的时间了？肯定是，不然罗伯特也不会冒雨匆忙把邮箱里的东西倒进麻袋。比洛多有些犹豫。那个邮局职员的存在令他十分烦恼。自打在春天闹了不愉快后，他都没和罗伯特说过话，而且无意去受羞辱。再说了，那里不仅有罗伯特一人，还有个邮差在他一旁，很可能是接替比洛多负责这片区域的人，他并不认识此人，但他最近开始怀疑这个人试图偷看塞格琳的信。

雨越来越大。罗伯特只想不再淋雨，便飞快地关上邮箱，把麻袋塞进面包车。他随时都会离开。比洛多只想把这首俳句寄出去：他强迫自己忘记自尊，大声喊住了那个邮局职员。罗伯特转过身，看到了他。比洛多挥动着手里的信，奔下台阶，跑到积满雨水的街上。另一个邮差挥着手臂，说了什么，只是他没听清。就在此时，汽车喇叭声划破了天空，紧跟着是猛烈的碰撞。

世界在比洛多周围缓慢地旋转，感觉像是置身梦中。他在空中翻了几圈，很想知道他这是怎么了，然后又是一次撞击，整个世界再次在他的背部下方变得稳定、沉重和坚硬。天空是灰蒙蒙的，雷声不绝于耳，大雨浇在他的眼睛上。他想动动身体，却根本做不到，这才发现他浑身疼得厉害。一个人出现在他和暴雨之间。那张脸很熟悉，是罗伯特。随即又出现了一张脸，是那个邮差，这张脸也很熟悉，只是熟悉的原因并不相同——这是他自己的脸。那个邮差的脸属于以前的比洛多，那个比洛多的样貌尚未改变，脸刮得很干净，眼神清澈。

从前的他正低头瞧着现在的他。

第二十三章

　　他怎么可能一边躺在积满水的柏油碎石路上，一边从上方看着他自己？这是魔术吗？比洛多迫切希望在还来得及的时候解开这个谜团，一个声音在他的内心中低声念出了格朗普雷诗集开头和结尾所用的那首俳句，给了他一个答案：

时光若流水，

彷徨复彷徨，

恋恋崎岖礁石上。

　　就是这么回事。历史重演了。时间在他身上耍了卑劣的伎俩。格朗普雷垂死挣扎的时刻打着旋儿撞击在岩石上，随波逐流，时间被困在了旋涡中，形成了一个圈，困住了比洛多。

　　格朗普雷是否也有这样的感觉？他在写下那首俳句的时候，是否知晓这首诗预言了未来？

　　生命是不断重复的。比洛多搁浅在了时间的浅滩上。他此刻处在剧痛之中，却还是大笑起来，这简直叫人难以置信，又荒唐至极。他笑了起来，吞下雨水，他越是笑，这一切在他看来就越是可笑。然后，一个硬块卡在了他的喉咙里，他再也笑不出来了。整件事根本不值得一笑。事实上，他的遭遇充满悲剧色彩：他终究还是难逃一死，得不到任何慰藉，而且，他即便知道死是解脱，却还是无法从中找到安慰，因为他只需要看看另一个比洛多，看着他急切地望着他手中的那封信，他就知道，眼下的情况并不是结局，现在轮到另一个比洛多了，循环还在继续，载着他走向死亡，然后，会有新的接替者出现，循环往复，永不停止。残忍的是，比洛多已经迎来了不断循环的死亡，这个诅咒是无法避免的，除非……

除非可以保留那封信……阻止它被冲进下水道……他要一直举着那封信，好让另一个比洛多拿到信、读过后决定把信寄出去，这样一来，他的生活或许就将进入另一条不同的时间河流中……

至于那之后，谁知道会怎么样？说不定循环会终止，也可以避开诅咒。他使出仅余的力气，运用到右手上，紧紧捏住那封信。他闭上眼，集中意志力，一个异乎寻常的影像出现在他的脑海中——那是一个红色的圆环，更确切地说，那是个旋转着的火圈。

依然是那个遭到诅咒的圆圈。蛇咬着自己的尾巴，时间在吞噬自己。

忽然之间，比洛多的心里浮现出了几个模糊的音节，那是格朗普雷临死前的遗言——换鞋 ①。他当时以为听到的是这两个字。他当时没听懂，但现在全明白了。

"禅圆。"他呻吟着说，这时，最后一点生命从他的身体里流逝了。

---

① 原文中，"in-sole"（鞋底），与"Enso"（禅圆）的发音相近。
——编者注

The Peculiar Life of a Lonely Postman

To Louise and Guy

Swirling like water

against rugged rocks

time goes around and around

Beech Street, rue des Hêtres, was for the most part lined with maples. Glancing down the road, one saw a double row of four- or five-storey apartment buildings, with outside staircases providing access to the upper floors. The street had 115 of those staircases, which added up to 1,495 steps. Bilodo knew this because he had counted and re-counted them, since he climbed every one of those stairs every single morning. These 1,495 steps, each with an average height of 20 centimetres, made for a total of 299 metres. More than one and a half times the height of Place Ville-Marie. He in fact hoofed it up the equivalent of the Eiffel Tower day after day, rain or shine, not to mention the fact that he had to go back down, too. Bilodo did not view this vertical marathon as an achievement. It was a daily challenge rather; without it, his life would have seemed quite flat to him. Considering himself a kind of athlete, he felt a particular kinship with long-distance hikers, those bold trekking specialists, and felt the odd twinge of regret that, among all the admirable forms of endurance sports, there wasn't a category for stair climbers. He would almost certainly have put up a good show in the 1,500 steps or 250-metre ascent–descent. If at the Olympic Games there had been a stair-scaling event, Bilodo would have stood an excellent chance of qualifying, perhaps even of mounting the ultimate, glorious top step of the podium.

In the meantime, he was a postman.

He was twenty-seven years old.

— ✉ —

Bilodo had been tracing the same postal route in Saint-Janvier-des-Âmes for five years now. He had actually moved into the heart of this working-class district so as to be closer to his job. During all those years of loyal service, he had missed only one day of work to attend the funeral of his parents, who had died in a funicular accident in Quebec City. He could be described as a steady employee.

In the morning, at the Depot, he began by sorting his post for the day. He had to arrange all the envelopes and parcels into the order they were to be delivered and tie them into bundles, which a postal employee in a van would transport to secure boxes along the route. Bilodo managed to carry out this tedious task with exceptional speed. He had his own sorting method, which was inspired by both the card-dealing technique of croupiers and the expertise of knife-throwers: like blades flung with lethal accuracy, the envelopes would leave his hand, fly towards the target, and slip into the appropriate pigeonhole. He rarely missed. This remarkable skill allowed him to finish well before the others – a good thing, too, because he could then escape. Bilodo couldn't think of anything more exciting than taking off, decamping, drinking in the fresh air and savouring the fragrance of a new day while walking about in the morning hours without anyone telling him what to do.

It wasn't all roses, of course. There were those blasted advertising flyers to be delivered; the backaches, the sprains and other run-of-the-mill injuries; there were the crushing summer heatwaves, the autumn rains that left you soaked to the skin, the black ice in winter, which turned the city into a perilous ice palace, and the cold that could be biting, just like the dogs for that matter – a postman's natural enemies. But the moral satisfaction of knowing oneself to be indispensable to the community made up for these drawbacks. Bilodo felt he took part in the life of the neighbourhood, that he had a discreet but essential role in it. For him, delivering post was a mission he accomplished conscientiously, knowing he contributed in this way to the maintenance of order in the universe. He wouldn't have wanted to swap places with anyone in the world. Except perhaps with another postman.

— ✉ —

Bilodo usually had lunch at the Madelinot, a restaurant located not far from the Depot, and, after his dessert, he'd spend a bit of time doing calligraphy, that art of fine penmanship, which he practised as an amateur. Getting out his exercise book and nibs, he would settle himself at the counter and transcribe a few words from a newspaper or an item from the menu. He'd grow absorbed in the choreographic movements of the nib on the paper, waltz among the downstrokes and upstrokes of Italian hand, perform volts with opulent uncial or cross swords with Gothic script, fancying himself as one of those worthy medieval copyist monks who lived on ink alone, ruining their eyes, their fingers freezing but their soul aglow.

Bilodo's colleagues at the Depot were baffled. As they flocked noisily into the Madelinot at lunchtime, they jeered at his calligraphic efforts, calling them scribbles. Bilodo didn't take offence, because they were his friends, and all they were really guilty of was ignorance. Unless one was an informed and devoted enthusiast like himself, how could one possibly savour the subtle beauty of a pen stroke, the delicately balanced proportions of a well-executed line? The only person who seemed capable of appreciating these things was Tania, the waitress. She was always pleasant and appeared genuinely interested in what he was doing and told him she thought it was beautiful. A sensitive young woman, to be sure. Bilodo liked her very much. He always left her a large tip. If he'd been a little more observant, he would have noticed she often watched him from her spot near the till and at dessert time always served him the biggest piece of pie. But he didn't notice. Or did he choose not to?

Bilodo no longer looked at other women since Ségolène had come into his life.

— ✉ —

Bilodo lived on the tenth floor of a high-rise in a one-bedroom apartment decorated with film posters, which he shared with his goldfish, Bill. In the evening he played Halo or Call of Duty, and then ate his dinner, a ready meal, while watching TV. He hardly ever went out. Only the odd Friday, when Robert became too insistent. Robert, a fellow postal worker, was assigned to the clearing of postboxes, and was also his best friend. Robert went out often, almost every night, but Bilodo rarely agreed to come along because he didn't really care for those smoky nightspots, those earsplitting raves, and those clubs with nude dancers his friend dragged him off to. He preferred to stay at home, far from the hustle and bustle of the world and from female posteriors – more so than ever since Ségolène had entered his life.

Anyhow, he had better things to do with his evenings. Bilodo was extremely busy in his apartment at night. After the TV and the dishes, he bolted the door and indulged in his secret vice.

Bilodo was an unusual postman.

Among the thousands of soulless pieces of paper he delivered on his rounds, he occasionally came across a personal letter – a less and less common item in this era of email, and all the more fascinating for being so rare. When that happened, Bilodo felt as excited as a prospector spotting a gold nugget in his pan. He did not deliver that letter. Not right away. He took it home and steamed it open. That's what kept him so busy at night in the privacy of his apartment.

Bilodo was an inquisitive postman.

He himself never received personal post. He would've liked to but didn't have anyone to whom he was close enough to correspond. He used to send letters to himself, but the experience had been a disappointment. He'd gradually stopped, and didn't really miss it; he didn't miss himself. More alluring by far were letters from others. Real letters, written by real people who preferred the sensual act of writing by hand, the delightfully languorous anticipation of the reply, to the reptilian coldness of the keyboard and instantaneity of the Internet – people for whom the act of writing was a deliberate choice and in some cases, one sensed, a matter of principle, a stand taken in favour of a lifestyle not quite so determined by the race against time and the obligation to perform.

There were those comical letters Doris T. wrote from Maria in the Gaspé Peninsula to her sister Gwendoline to fill her in on the local gossip, and those heart-rending ones Richard L., detained in the Port Cartier prison, sent to his young son, Hugo. There were those long mystical epistles Sister Régine of the Congrégation du Saint-Rosaire in Rimouski dispatched to her old friend Germaine, and those erotic little tales Laetitia D., a young nurse temporarily exiled in the Yukon, composed for her lonely fiancé, and also those strange missives in which a mysterious O. gave advice to a certain N. on how to safely invoke various supernatural beings. There was anything and everything, coming from here, there, and everywhere: letters from close relatives and faraway correspondents, letters from beer tasters comparing notes, from globetrotters writing to their mothers, from retired steam locomotive firemen listing their bumps and bruises. There were those overly reassuring letters servicemen dispatched from Afghanistan to their anxious wives, and those worried words uncles wrote to their nieces concerning secrets that shouldn't be revealed for anything in the world, and those Dear John or Dear Mary letters in which circus acrobats in Las Vegas broke up with their former lovers, and there were even hate letters crammed with insults spilling out onto the envelope.

But above all there were love letters. Because even after Valentine's Day, love remained the most common denominator, the subject linking the greatest number of pens. Love in every grammatical form and every possible tone, dished up in every imaginable shape: passionate letters or courteous ones, sometimes suggestive and sometimes chaste, either calm or dramatic, occasionally violent, often lyrical, and especially moving when the feelings were expressed in simple terms, and never quite so touching as when the emotions hid between the lines, burning away almost invisibly behind a screen of innocuous words.

Once he'd read and reread the letter of the day, had savoured it down to the very marrow, Bilodo made a photocopy of it for his records. He put this in a folder, the colour of which corresponded to the subject, which he placed in a fireproof filing cabinet. He would slip the original letter back into its envelope, deftly seal it, and drop it into the addressee's letterbox the next day as if nothing had happened. He had been practising this clandestine activity for two years now. It was a crime, he was well aware of that, but guilt paled into insignificance beside supreme curiosity. No one was hurt by it, after all, and he himself didn't risk much as long as he continued to be careful. Who was going to worry that the delivery of a letter was twenty-four hours late? And, for a start, who could know it was late?

— ✉ —

Bilodo intercepted letters from about thirty correspondents in this way. All together they formed a kind of soap opera with multiple plots. Or rather half of a soap opera, whose other half, the one of the "outgoing post", was unfortunately unavailable to him. But he liked to make up that other part, to draft elaborate replies he never posted, and when another letter arrived he was often amazed to see how naturally it fitted in with his own secret reply.

That's how it was. Bilodo lived vicariously. To the dullness of real life he preferred his infinitely more colourful, more thrilling, interior serial drama. And of all the clandestine letters that constituted this fascinating little virtual world, none mobilized or enchanted him more than the ones from Ségolène.

····· ·····
3
····· ·····

Ségolène lived at Pointe-à-Pitre in Guadeloupe and wrote regularly to a certain Gaston Grandpré, who rented an apartment on rue des Hêtres. Bilodo had been intercepting her letters for two years now, and whenever he spotted one while sorting his post, he always experienced the same shock, the same shiver of awe. He would quietly slip that letter inside his jacket and only allow himself to show any emotion once he was alone on the road, turning the envelope over and over, fingering the exciting promise. He could have opened it right away and revelled in the words it concealed, but he'd rather wait. All he granted himself was the fleeting pleasure of inhaling the fragrance of oranges wafting up from the letter before bravely putting it back in his pocket, and he kept it there all day, against his heart, resisting temptation, drawing out the pleasure until evening, until after the washing up was done. Then the time had come. He would burn a few drops of citrus oil, light a few candles, put on a disc of dreamy Norwegian jazz, and then, at last, he unsealed the envelope, gently reached into its inner fold, and read:

Under clear water
the newborn baby
swims like a playful otter

Bilodo could see it. He vividly saw that stark-naked baby in the aqueous luminescence of the postnatal swimming pool while it swam towards him as if he were its mother, as if it were swimming towards the outstretched arms of a mermaid who would be its mother and who was watching him with deep blue flabber-gasted-salamander eyes. It didn't know it couldn't swim, hadn't forgotten how to yet. It had no idea water was dangerous, a foreign element, that it could drown in it. The baby was ignorant of all this, it just moved about, followed its instinct, kept its mouth closed, and simply swam. Bilodo saw that young pinniped clearly – that funny underwater gnome with the crinkly features of infants and nostrils ringed with bubbles, as it glided through the voluptuous water, and Bilodo laughed because it was unexpected, because it was amusing, touching. And he thought he was floating too. He could hear the water buzzing against his eardrums.

He felt as though he was in that swimming pool together with that baby. For such was the suggestive power of all those strange little poems Ségolène wrote: they made you feel things, made you see them.

The letters from the Guadeloupean woman contained nothing else. Always a single sheet of paper on which was written a single poem. It wasn't much, yet it was generous, since those poems nourished you as much as a whole novel – they were long in your soul, where they echoed forever. Bilodo learned them by heart and recited them to himself on his morning round. He treasured them up in the top drawer of his bedside table and liked spreading them around him at night, constructing a kind of mystical circle, and rereading them one after the other...

Slowly flowing sky
breakup of the clouds
icebergs that have lost their way

Leaving its harp shell
the spider crab, bungee queen
takes the final plunge

A hammering in the streets
shutters are nailed down
the cyclone draws near

Nighttime out at sea
the shark yawns indolently
munches a moonfish

Dancing, swaying bowls
as the tablecloth
billows in the summer breeze

Ségolène's poems, as different as they were from each other, were all alike in their form, since they always consisted of three lines: two of five syllables and one of seven, adding up to seventeen syllables, no more, no less. Always that same mysterious structure, as though governed by a code. Because Bilodo sensed that this consistency had to have a specific purpose, he'd puzzled over it until the day when, after months of foggy surmising, he happened to discover what it was all about. It was on a Saturday morning. He was having breakfast at the Madelinot while reading the entertainment supplement of a newspaper. Suddenly the sight, at the top of a page, of three written lines that seemed to form a short poem made him choke on his coffee. The poem had two lines of five syllables and one of seven. The verse was disappointing in other respects; it simply gave an ironic commentary on current affairs. It was nothing like the living fragments of eternity created by Ségolène. But the column's title was revealing: "THE SATURDAY

HAIKU". Bilodo rushed home, combed the dictionary and found the word:

Haiku/'haiku:/ n. (pl. same) 1 a type of very short Japanese poem, having three parts, usu. 17 syllables, and often about a subject in nature. 2 an imitation of this in another language. [Japanese]

So that was it. That's what the Guadeloupean woman's poems were. Since then, Bilodo had been able to consult numerous books containing haiku at the library – books translated from the Japanese, grouping together well-known authors such as Matsuo Bashō, Taneda Santōka, Nagata Kōi and Kobayashi Issa, but none of the poems by these men produced the effect of Ségolène's, none of them carried him off to as faraway a place or made him see things as clearly or feel them as acutely.

No doubt Ségolène's penmanship contributed greatly to this exceptional magic, for she expressed herself in a more delicate, more graceful Italian hand than Bilodo had ever had the good fortune to admire. It was a rich, imaginative handwriting, with deep downstrokes and celestial upstrokes embellished with opulent loops and precise drops – a clean, flowing script, admirably well-proportioned with its perfect thirty-degree slant and flawless interletter spacing. Ségolène's writing was a sweet scent for the eye, an elixir, an ode. It was a graphic symphony, an apotheosis. It was so beautiful it made you weep. Having read somewhere that handwriting was a reflection of a person's soul, Bilodo readily concluded that Ségolène's soul must be incomparably pure. If angels wrote, surely it was like this.

Bilodo knew that Ségolène was a primary school teacher at Pointe-à-Pitre, and he also knew she was beautiful. He'd seen this in a picture she'd posted to Grandpré, very likely in exchange for one of his own, since the back of the photo carried this handwritten line: "Delighted to have made your photographic acquaintance. Now it is my turn. Here I am with my pupils." The snap showed her in the middle of a group of smiling school-children, but only her smile mattered to Bilodo's eyes, and her emerald gaze crashed deep into his own like a wave against a cliff, reverberating there like an echo. He had digitized and printed that photo, then put it, framed, on his bedside table above the drawer where he kept her haiku. Now he could contemplate Ségolène every night before going to sleep and soon afterward dream about her: her smile, her eyes, and all the other marvels of her appearance, about romantic seaside strolls in her company, with Marie-Galante looming in the twilight and torrents of orangey clouds scudding across the sky while the wind raked their hair – unless the world of haiku got involved in his oneiric fantasies, for then he dreamt instead that he was bungee jumping with her, that they fell together at the end of an extremely long elastic before diving into a fragrant ocean, slipping between corals among moonfish and baby amphibians, amid puzzled sharks.

$$= \text{✉} =$$

Bilodo was in love as he'd never imagined one could possibly be. The hold Ségolène had gained over his soul was so enormous it sometimes worried him – he was afraid his life wasn't his own any more. But the alchemical reading of a few haiku quickly transmuted his distress into bliss, and then he thanked his lucky star for favouring him like this, for having placed the Guadeloupean beauty in his path. The only shadow over his happiness was the jealousy stirring within him when he remembered that Ségolène's letters were really intended for someone else. Whenever he finished reading a new poem, he felt the sting of envy as he resealed the envelope and slipped it the next day into the slot at the apartment of that guy, Gaston Grandpré, his rival. How had he met Ségolène? What was he to her? The note on the back of the picture and the general tenor of the poems didn't suggest anything more than friendship, which cheered Bilodo up somewhat, but even so it was for Grandpré, the lucky man, that the letters were meant. Bilodo occasionally caught a glimpse of him standing in his doorway. Bearded, messy-looking, his hair unkempt, always wearing an extravagant red dressing gown, he invariably gave the impression he'd been up all night. A grouch with the air of a mad scientist about him. A grungy oddball. How did he react, Bilodo wondered, when he found another letter from her on his doormat? Did he rush to quench his thirst at the oasis of her words? Did he feel the same thrill? Did Ségolène's poems make him see things, too? The same things they conjured up for Bilodo? And what did he write in reply?

In the afternoon, when Bilodo walked past the Madelinot again on his way home, he sometimes spotted Grandpré inside, sipping a cup of coffee and scribbling in a notepad, looking inspired. Did he write poetry? Bilodo would have given anything to be able to do the same. He would have liked to reply to Ségolène's letters, just as he did to those from his other unwitting pen pals, but felt incapable of doing so, since the only way one could possibly respond to her lovely haiku was with another, just as beautifully crafted. And how could Bilodo, whom the mere word poetry intimidated, have managed that? Could a humble postman become a poet overnight? Could an ostrich be expected to start playing the banjo? Did snails ride bicycles? He actually tried once or twice early on and turned out a few pitiful attempts at verse, but had been overcome with shame and had never dared do it again, because he feared he might strike a blow to the very core of Poetry and indirectly tarnish Ségolène's sacred creations. Did Grandpré have that rare gift? Did he write haiku?

Was he aware at least how fortunate he was? Did he feel even a quarter of what Bilodo felt for Ségolène? Or even one-tenth?

— ✉ —

Linked to Bilodo's worship of Ségolène was a strong fascination with the blessed land of her birth, the natural setting in the heart of which she shone. He often raided the travel shelves in bookstores and spent hours on the Internet filling his brain with anything relating to Guadeloupe: the archipelago's geology; recipes of the local cuisine; the musical tradition; the manufacture of rum; the area's history; fishing techniques; botany; architecture – he greedily lapped it all up. Little by little, Bilodo became a specialist where the "butterfly island" was concerned, although he'd never set foot on it. He could of course have gone there, travelled there and seen Guadeloupe with his own eyes, but he had never seriously considered it because the idea unnerved him, incurable homebody that he was. Bilodo had no desire to physically visit Guadeloupe – he only wanted to get a detailed picture of it in his mind so as to feed his dreams and set them in a realistic landscape that would show Ségolène to advantage. That way he could fantasize about her in high definition, with all the necessary mental technology.

He dreamt of her cycling down the Allée Dumanoir between the royal palms that proudly lined the avenue. He dreamt of her strolling on La Darse in the afternoon when the lycée was out, or going shopping at the Marché Saint-Antoine, sauntering about in the large covered market among multicoloured stalls piled high with figues-pomme bananas and yams, sweet potatoes and chili peppers, pineapples, cherimoyas, malangas, and star fruit – not forgetting the spices, cinnamon, colombo powder, saffron, vanilla, bayberry, and curry, whose mingled aromas stirred the senses, and next to these the punches and syrups, candy and basketwork, flowers, parakeets, and brooms, beside potions, brews that bring relief and fidelity, wealth or endless love, and other magic philtres intended to cure all the ills of the world.

He dreamt of her every night, and the setting of these ethereal films, in which Ségolène played the lead, was the whole island of Guadeloupe with its winding roads and sugar-cane fields, its steep paths cutting through orchid-studded jungles dense with giant ferns, its mist-crowned mountains with strings of cascades and waterfalls dangling down the mossy, green sides. And its towering La Soufrière, dormant but ever threatening, its luminous villages with red sheet-metal roofs and cemeteries filled with black-and-white-checkered graves decorated with seashells. Its carnival, music, gwoka players, she-devils dressed all in red and other dancers in many-hued costumes wriggling their hips to the beat of bola drums while the rum flowed freely.

Guadeloupe with its mangrove swamps and guava, islands and islets, manta rays gliding on the surface of the water, its lacy coral, mullet, grouper and flying fish, the fishermen of Les Saintes, their heads shaded by salakos, repairing their nets. The jagged, ocean-whipped, limestone coastline of the north of Basse-Terre. Then, suddenly, surprisingly tranquil coves, blond beaches, and Ségolène swimming in the rollers of a sea as turquoise as her eyes, and the sun hastening to win back that second Venus as soon as she emerged from the waves and returned to the beach, treading it gracefully – naked and yet modest with water clinging to her breasts in beads and streaming over the downy gold of her belly.

Bilodo dreamt, and wished for nothing else; he wanted only to continue on like this, to keep savouring the dazzling dreams and ecstatic visions Ségolène's words conjured up for him. His only desire was that the pleasant status quo might endure, that nothing would disturb his quiet bliss. And nothing did, until the fateful day when the accident happened.

········· ·········
5
········· ·········

It was a stormy morning in late August. The sky hung heavy and thundered in the distance but couldn't make up its mind to spill it all out, but this didn't disturb Bilodo in the least since he had faith in the impermeability of the sturdy raincoat provided by the Post Office. At a determined pace no dreary skies could have slowed, he was making his way up and down rue des Hêtres, tackling one staircase after another, when he ran into his friend Robert, who was just transferring the contents of a postbox to his van.

They rarely met up like this, because the clearing of this particular box was generally done before Bilodo passed by, but Robert explained he had overslept after a wild night with a certain Brenda, a fantastic girl he'd met in a bar. After their hellos and some friendly banter, Bilodo wanted to get going again, but Robert held him back – he had much more to say on the subject of his brand new flame and suggested they double date that very evening with Brenda and a friend of hers, a girl with great erotic potential. Bilodo sighed. Robert's relentless efforts to set him up with a girlfriend annoyed him. His co-worker disapproved of his endless bachelorhood, considered it unhygienic, and had ironically nicknamed him "Libido". He'd taken it upon himself to act as a go-between and tried to mate Bilodo with anything that moved, registering him without his knowledge with online dating agencies and placing crude ads in his name along with his phone number in the sexy personal ads of trendy magazines.

All these initiatives annoyed Bilodo. He didn't dare answer the phone any more, and his voicemail was constantly clogged. But he couldn't hold it against Robert, because he knew he meant well. He was only going to all that trouble in order to help him, after all. Robert overdid it, as always, it was typical of him, but he was nevertheless the best friend he had in the world, wasn't he? Bilodo tried to appreciate him just the way he was – with his vulgarity, selfishness, hypocrisy, opportunism, compulsive exaggerating, and bad breath.

Although willing to forgive Robert for these trivial character flaws, he nonetheless hated the kind of random orgy he was being invited to. Since Robert wasn't the sort to take no for an answer, he quickly needed to come up with some valid excuse, one that wouldn't sound too lame, and that's what he was busy doing when the storm broke.

There was a sudden clap of thunder as if a colossal bag of crisps had split open overhead, and the sky cracked. The rain came down in sheets, limiting visibility to a couple of metres. Robert hurriedly flung his bag into the van and invited Bilodo to hop in so he wouldn't get soaked. The postman agreed that it would be better to let the storm blow over, so he accepted and walked around the vehicle. Just then a shout from the other side of the street drew his attention. Bilodo turned around and spotted Grandpré, Ségolène's penfriend, the man with the perennial dressing gown, on his third-storey landing exactly opposite.

Opening his umbrella, Grandpré tore down the stairs, brandishing a letter he no doubt wanted to post before Robert drove off. Bilodo watched him stepping out carelessly onto the road, which had already turned into a rising river. Without bothering to check that the way was clear, Grandpré ran towards them, hailed them, asked them to wait, and didn't see the truck coming, bearing down on them, ploughing through the downpour. Bilodo stretched out his arm, called out an inarticulate warning to Grandpré while the truck's horn blared, but it was too late. The brakes screeched, the wheels skidded on the wet road, then there was a thud. The vehicle seemed to stop instantly, as though all its kinetic energy had been passed on to Grandpré who was catapulted into the air like a big rag doll and then crashed down with a limp thwack close to the pavement, ten metres further on.

Cars came to a halt. The world seemed to stand still. For a few moments, the only sounds were the hum of idling motors, the crackle of the rain beating down on the asphalt and drumming on the roofs of the cars. Grandpré was now just a formless heap one could have taken for an armful of laundry that had slipped from someone's grip, if there hadn't been those shudders and dreadful spasms rocking him. Robert, the first to react, moved forward. Bilodo followed him, and they knelt down next to Grandpré, who lay there helpless, broken, his limbs bent at preposterous angles, his bushy beard spattered with thick blood that the rain, however heavy, didn't wash away. The poor guy was conscious. He stared at Robert, then at Bilodo, with a stunned look of disbelief, his eyelashes fluttering like the wings of twin butterflies, his gaze blurred by the downpour. His right hand still held the letter he'd been so eager to post, and Bilodo saw it was addressed to Ségolène.

A reddening stream rushed down the gutter. He wasn't going to make it. He desperately struggled for breath and Bilodo thought this was it, he was dying, but Grandpré began to let out odd gasps. Dumbfounded, Bilodo realised the dying man was laughing. It was definitely laughter – raucous and hollow, colourless, ghostly. Bilodo shivered and noticed he wasn't the only one: the other witnesses seemed just as disconcerted by the sinister laughter bursting forth from a dying throat. Grandpré went on laughing for a bit, as though at a painful joke. Then he stopped as he choked in a fit of coughing and spat out scarlet sputters.

Turning his head with great effort, he gazed at the bloody letter in his hand while his fingers tightened on the envelope. Grandpré closed his eyes, clenched his teeth; he looked as if he were focusing whatever strength he had left on that last expression of will, that final gesture of holding the letter. And suddenly he spoke, uttered a few words, but so faintly that only Bilodo and Robert, bent over him, could catch them: he murmured something indistinct that sounded like "in-sole". Then, all at once, it was the end. His eyelids opened wide and his pupils dilated, glazed over. Grandpré's eyes filled with rain, formed tiny lakes, while his last, enigmatic word lingered in Bilodo's head. What did that "in-sole" signify? What had the dead man meant? For a fleeting moment Bilodo was tempted to look inside Grandpré's shoes to check if something was hidden there, but then he wondered if he wasn't misinterpreting the deceased's utterance. Taking into account the harrowing groans accompanying it, shouldn't one assume it to mean 'an-swer' instead – a reference to that final leap into the unknown, to that imminent dive into the mystery of the hereafter the dying man was knowingly getting ready for?

At that moment, Bilodo saw that the letter was no longer in the dead man's hand. Grandpré must have let go of it at the moment of death, and the letter had slipped into the gutter where the swift current had immediately swept it away. Bilodo spotted it drifting downstream between the feet of gaping onlookers, sucked away from the funereal circle by the whirling water as it rushed towards a sewer-grate cascade. Galvanized, he dashed after it, jostling the witnesses to the tragedy. He knew he had to get that letter back at all costs. He ran, bent down, stretched out his hand to catch it. He felt his arm grow longer, his fingers extending inordinately, and reaching it... but a millisecond too late – the sewer swallowed the letter. Carried along by his momentum, Bilodo stumbled and landed flat on his back in the cold water. A flash of lightning streaked the sky at the very moment an equally blinding realisation illuminated Bilodo: with the disappearance of that letter, which the bowels of the earth had swallowed up, his only link with Ségolène had just been severed.

Bilodo was in a dismal mood when he set off the next day, and it seemed to him as if the sun was in mourning, too, as if it dispensed only the cold kind of light you saw in old black-and-white movies. When he got to rue des Hêtres, he paused on the pavement, at the spot where Grandpré had fallen, and it distressed him to find that not a single trace of the tragedy remained, not even a tiny puddle of blood. The rain had washed it all away.

The haunting image of that letter gobbled up by the sewer kept returning to Bilodo's mind. He felt bad he hadn't been more alert. If only he could have caught it, read it, and found out at least what Grandpré wrote to Ségolène. Would he have posted it afterwards, he wondered? Most likely, if only to delay the inevitable. But it was no use thinking about it. Ségolène wasn't going to get that letter, so she wouldn't reply to it, and Bilodo would never again read her poems. Grandpré's death put an end to that precious correspondence, the spice of his life. Was there anything more awful than being powerless?

A little while later, as he went down the street in the opposite direction, Bilodo arrived at the door of the deceased and slipped the usual bills and advertising flyers through the letter slot, knowing full well it was pointless, the post would just pile up on the other side until perhaps a "Request to Discontinue Service" reached the Post Office.

Pensive, he pictured the interior of that unknown apartment, where from now on silence reigned and time stagnated, where the only traces of Grandpré's earthly journey were some furniture, some objects, a few clothes hanging on motionless hangers, a few photographs, a few written works.

— ✉ —

Grandpré's death didn't cause much commotion in the neighbour-hood because people barely knew him. At the Madelinot, Tania laid a carnation on the table he usually occupied when he came in for a coffee. That was all. So this was how we departed this world, Bilodo reflected: by accident, without making waves or leaving a lingering trail, like a swallow flashing across the sky, and as quickly forgotten as a squirrel inadvertently run over on the road.

That's how it was.

Nothing appeared to have changed. Bilodo got up at dawn and went to work, had lunch at the Madelinot, then went home. His existence seemed to pursue its untroubled course, but only outwardly, for below the surface of the glassy sea that was his daily routine, a subtle change was taking place almost without him noticing.

At first, it was just a feeling of weariness, a gloomy mood he put down to the changing of the season, to the days growing shorter, a harbinger of autumn. But soon the symptoms of a deeper malaise began to show up: one night, while looking over his old clandestine correspondences, Bilodo realised that this activity, so exciting in former days, bored him all of a sudden. His favourite soap opera fell flat; none of its plots held his interest any more. The dramatic events of other people's lives no longer fascinated him.

The next day, at the Depot, he was unable to sort the post with his usual ease. He missed the target every second time, so he had to resign himself to proceeding in the conventional way. He was twenty minutes late setting off and hoped the morning air would buck him up, but he could feel his energy fading after walking just three miserable kilometres. It was even worse when he had to pit himself against the rue des Hêtres staircases: he'd merely got to the twenty-fourth one when he needed to stop to take a breather, and only reached the end of the street by a violent effort of will, after he'd allowed himself as many as six breaks. What was happening to him?

Was he coming down with the flu?

When he arrived at the Madelinot, he found he had no appetite whatsoever, he who normally wolfed down his food, and ordered only vegetable soup, which he didn't even finish. He didn't bother getting out his calligraphy tools – he didn't feel like it – and immediately continued his round to make up for lost time. He was in an unusual state of mental confusion. Inattentive, preoccupied with he wasn't quite sure what, he crossed an intersection at a red light and came within an inch of being knocked over by a car. But he'd only escaped Charybdis to run into Scylla: soon after, as he dropped some advertising flyers into the letterbox of a house, Bilodo was attacked by a dog on a chain. The one-eyed animal, actually called Polyphemus according to the sign on its kennel, bit him viciously in his right calf and would only let go when its master, who'd been alerted by the howls, whacked it with a shovel. That's what happened when the gods were against you.

— ✉ —

By the time the business with the dog had been dealt with – the anti-rabies vaccine administered and Bilodo's wound dressed and bandaged after he'd spent six hours at the emergency department – when that wretched odyssey had finally ended, it was late. On his way home in a taxi, Bilodo felt like doling out a few good whacks with a shovel, too. The sharp shooting pains in his leg only intensified his fury. He wanted to rebel, but what could he possibly do against the curse that had been stalking him this whole dreadful day where everything was going wrong? Once home, he bolted the door of his cocoon and hobbled up and down the living room in search of an outlet for his anger. He turned on the computer and started venting his rage on the wicked insurgents of the planet Xion. Maltreating his console, he massacred hordes of tentacular creatures, reached the game's higher level, achieved a record score, but didn't succeed in soothing the rage that twisted his guts.

Eventually he went to bed, dead tired, and found a bit of peace by gazing at Ségolène's picture. He imagined the lovely Guadeloupean woman opening her letterbox every morning, hoping to spot that reply from Grandpré, which never came. He briefly thought he might write to her to let her know her penfriend had passed away, but he couldn't do that of course – it would have meant betraying himself, admitting he'd been guilty of an indiscretion. How long would Ségolène wait, he wondered, before giving up?

— ✉ —

It happened during the thunderstorm, on rue des Hêtres, right after the accident, but instead of Grandpré, it was Ségolène who lay helpless on the wet asphalt. She was covered with blood, dying. The young woman held out a trembling hand to Bilodo, implored him not to forget her... and he woke with a start, gasping for breath, chilled to the bone. He had trouble reconnecting with reality because the nightmare lingered, kept forcing its morbid images on him. Anxious to dispel the dread that gripped him, Bilodo spread Ségolène's haiku around him to create a defensive circle against the crawling darkness. He began reading them out loud, like so many protective incantations, but it only deepened his distress because the words refused to generate the music he expected: as soon as they were uttered, the night soaked them up, and the comforting visions they should have produced failed to appear. The haiku proved to be sterile all of a sudden. With their neatly arranged lines on their single sheets like withered flowers in a herbarium, they were lifeless, merely exuded a faded scent.

Bilodo shook the pages, hoping to reactivate the magic, but only managed to crumple them. Even Ségolène's words let him down. And at that moment, for the first time in his life, really the very first time, he felt loneliness swooping down on him. It was like a huge wave submerging him, sending him down to the very depths of himself, driving him into the darkest reaches of the ocean depths, where an irresistible maelstrom swept him towards a monstrous, gaping chasm, a gigantic sewer grate, while he groped for something to cling to, anguished to the core of his soul.

Strangely lucid, Bilodo realised he wouldn't be able to go on living without Ségolène, he wouldn't survive, nothing would have meaning or importance any more, beauty and desire lost to him forever, peace of mind an abstract concept drifting somewhere in the distance along with all those other emotions he'd probably never feel, and he himself just a piece of wreckage. A ghost ship, with no one at the helm and no power, carried along by the briny currents until eventually Sargasso weeds slowed him, caught him in their viscous nets, invading the timber, weighing him down so much he would founder in them.

What a hideous prospect. Was the story going to end so stupidly? Shouldn't Bilodo do something, try to think of something? Could the shipwreck be averted? Was there a buoy to hang on to, a way to overcome helplessness, some method or other of warding off ill fortune, of preventing Ségolène from being cast out of his life?

It was then, when his distress was greatest, Bilodo hit upon an idea.

— ✉ —

It was a brilliant idea – original, inspired, so daring that Bilodo took fright and quickly put the lid back on. Because the idea was too crazy, too dangerously absurd, far too risky, and probably unworkable anyway. A wild, unwholesome idea only a crackpot could have seriously considered, which should be rejected and forgotten as quickly as possible, for fear it might proliferate. To concentrate his mind on something else, Bilodo picked up his game console and launched a violent attack on the insurgents of Xion, but the idea refused to be evicted, kept scratching under the floor tiles, demanded to be allowed to spring into the light. And finally, tired of resisting, Bilodo resigned himself to examining it again.

Perhaps the plan wasn't totally crazy after all. It was absolutely terrifying, fraught with psychological danger, but might not be impossible to carry out. If there was still a chance of re-tying the thread and finding his way back to Ségolène, this was definitely the way. And just when a pale new day was breaking, Bilodo looked up: he understood he had no other option, he had to at least give it a try.

The breaking of the window was muffled by the thick, coarse towel. Straining all his senses, Bilodo listened for some reaction from the neighbouring doors and landings, probed the darkness in the alleyway down below, but nothing stirred. He pressed against the shattered pane so the fragments fell inside. Bilodo put his hand through the hole, found the bolt, and stepped inside the door, that of Grandpré's apartment on the alleyway side, then quickly closed it behind him. He was inside. He'd done it.

A sickly sweet odour prickled his nostrils. He was in the kitchen. He switched on his torch and moved forward, making himself as light as possible, trying to levitate above the creaking floorboards. The kitchen had neither table nor chairs. The smell came from the counter; something had been left there and was rotting in its package. Fish perhaps. After crossing the kitchen, Bilodo ventured into the passageway. Its floor was covered with a soft material – not a fitted carpet but a thin mattress of some kind, which appeared to be spread over the floors of the other rooms as well. There were three doors in the passageway. The first one opened into a bedroom, the second into a small bathroom. Straight ahead lay the living room, divided in two by a large screen of some sort. Bilodo stepped around a low, oddly shaped sculpture and slipped behind the partition, finding himself in front of a writing desk next to an armchair on casters. After he'd made sure the blinds were closed, he sat down in the armchair.

The torch's beam swept the desk, revealing a computer, a calendar, a few knickknacks, a dictionary, pens, and various papers. When he examined the papers, he immediately found what he'd come for: sheets covered with writing in a hand that could only be Grandpré's. In the top drawer he made an even more exciting discovery: poems by the deceased – haiku. A whole bundle of them. And right next to those, Bilodo discovered Ségolène's, her original haiku, of which he only had copies. And her picture too!

Overwhelmed with emotion, Bilodo admired that smile, so soothing to his soul, that gentle almond gaze that always set him dreaming, then he sniffed those blessed pages Ségolène's hand had held, that her perfume still clung to, and he kissed them. One moment of such bliss was enough to justify the risks he'd taken, but the job wasn't finished: continuing his search, Bilodo explored the other drawers. What he hoped to unearth more than anything else was a rough copy of Grandpré's last letter, the one the sewer had so disgracefully swallowed up, because that was the ultimate goal of the expedition. But he'd only just begun this search when he heard voices outside, people talking on the stairs. Bilodo jumped up, switched off the torch. Just neighbours walking up to a higher floor? Or police coming to nab the despicable burglar he was? Bilodo wasn't going to wait around to find out: he stuffed as many papers as he could into his jacket and bolted, crashing into that idiotic sculpture lying about in the living room. He fled through the back door, charged down the stairs, then shot at the speed of sound towards the exit of the alleyway. He didn't dare slow down until two blocks further on, once he knew for sure he wasn't being pursued. He forced himself to walk along as naturally as possible so as not to attract attention, but his heart kept skipping, beating like a drum.

— ✉ —

After a long shower to sluice away the sweat from the crime, Bilodo sat down at his table and reread Ségolène's haiku. He was delighted to discover that the little poems had regained their full vital power. Then, with Bill's discreet collusion, he looked over the other stolen papers, focusing especially on Grandpré's haiku, which confirmed what he'd long suspected: those two practised – had practised – a poetic exchange of some sort. Grandpré's haiku seemed quite different from Ségolène's, however. Not in form, but in spirit:

Swirling like water
against rugged rocks
time goes around and around

Smog in the city
it smokes far too much
emphysema guaranteed

They stir up the sea
sway the forest, draw
a low murmur from the earth

The rabbit's no fool
he bursts from the hole
where nobody lies in wait

To break through the horizon
look behind the set
meet and embrace Death

It was a more sombre kind of poetry than Ségolène's, more

dramatic, yet just as evocative: Grandpré's haiku made you see things too, although through a darkened lens. There were almost a hundred of them. The problem was that none were numbered. There was no indication of the order in which they'd been written or sent to Ségolène, no way of knowing which haiku was the last one, the one that never reached her.

Bilodo put the original of Ségolène's picture on his bedside table. Then, stretched out in the dark, he wondered what to do now that the first stage of his plan had been completed. Move on to phase two? Did he dare go through with his insane idea?

He fell asleep and had a strange dream. He dreamt of Gaston Grandpré, who lay dying in the middle of rue des Hêtres, just as he had in waking reality, except that the dying man didn't seem to be suffering in the least. On the contrary, he appeared to be having a good time and even gave Bilodo a knowing wink.

— ✉ —

At dawn, when Bilodo woke up, he decided to go through with the scheme. For the first time in five years he phoned in sick to the Post Office; then, without even taking time to have a cup of coffee, he bent over Grandpré's papers and studied his hand-writing, calling upon all his experience in calligraphy.

A thorough examination of the deceased's writings soon brought out an unusual feature. All over the sheets, sometimes right in the middle of a poem, a particular symbol had been drawn. It was a circle decorated to varying degrees with flourishes – could it be a stylized O? – which the author seemed to have obsessively scribbled here and there. Did that O have a particular meaning? Bilodo could only speculate. The penmanship itself was interesting, broad and vigorous. The stroke was strong, angular, boldly combining cursive and block letters, deeply scoring the paper. Pretty much the manly kind of handwriting Bilodo would've liked to have. Anyhow, he felt capable of imitating it. Choosing the same type of ballpoint pen that Grandpré had used, he made his first attempts, copying with a hesitant hand certain extracts from the deceased's poems.

The first notepad was used up shortly before noon. Bilodo's lunch consisted of a can of sardines which he ate standing as he trampled distractedly on the crumpled sheets. He set to work again, toiled until dusk, when he had to stop because of cramp. While massaging his sore wrist, he lost heart for a moment and considered giving up. But he pulled himself together at the thought of Ségolène waiting on her island and picked up his pen again, wielding it with fresh resolve.

Long after dark Bilodo finally deemed himself satisfied; he was able to produce a reasonably good imitation of the dead man's penmanship. So the second part of his plan had been completed, but he took care not to rejoice and prepared himself instead to face the next challenge, which was a sizeable one. Because the penmanship wasn't the whole story – he had to know what to write, too.

He'd deliberately avoided thinking about that aspect until then, choosing to concentrate on the task's technical side, but couldn't put it off any longer. Imitating Grandpré's hand was all very well, but, far more importantly, he needed to write what Grandpré would have written. Now Bilodo had to venture into unknown territory, into the foreign land of poetry, and manage somehow to compose a haiku that could pass as genuine in Ségolène's eyes.

— ✉ —

His aptitude for slipping into other people's words was of no help to him in this case – when dawn broke, all he'd been able to come up with was water, just that one word, inspired by Ségolène's last haiku about the aquatic baby. He couldn't think of anything intelligent to add. Of course one could team it up with a variety of qualifiers: clear water, flowing water, still water. But was that really poetic? He spent the morning in a trance, struggling to join something to his water that would transcend it. Fire water? Running water? Sparkling water?

Waterhead?

After giving himself permission to take a brief nap, he dreamt he was drowning. He woke up just in time to fill his lungs with air and went back to the blank page. Dish-water? Holy water? Water beetle? Waterworks?

Jump into the water?

Walk on water?

Then, having become captivated by the circular movements of Bill paddling around in his bowl, he got down to it and wrote: "A fish in water." That was one line of five syllables already. Almost a third of the tercet.

Bilodo gazed at the words with a critical eye, then crossed them all out.

Four words, and not a single one he was happy with. At this rate, he'd still be fishing for ideas at Christmas time.

He really must speed things up. How did one go about becoming a poet, Bilodo wondered. Was it something you could learn? Maybe there was a course called Haiku 101? The yellow pages didn't list any poetry schools, so who were you supposed to contact in an emergency? The Japanese Embassy? At least one thing was becoming clear: Bilodo needed to find out more about those infuriating haiku.

········ ·······

8

········ ·······

While combing the Japanese Literature section of the Central
Library, Bilodo hunted out a few highly instructive books, and it
didn't take him long to learn everything he'd always wanted to know
about haiku but had been afraid to ask. The principle was actually
quite simple: haiku sought to juxtapose the permanent and the
ephemeral. A good haiku ideally contained a reference to nature (kigo)
or to some reality not uniquely human. Sparing of words, precise, at
once complex and subtle, it shunned literary artifice and customary
poetic devices such as rhyme and metaphor. The art of haiku was
the art of the snapshot, of the detail. It could be about an episode in
someone's life, a memory, a dream, but it was above all a concrete
poem, appealing to the senses, not to ideas.

Bilodo was beginning to see the light. Even the epistolary haiku exchange Ségolène and Grandpré had practised took on a specific meaning: it was a renku or "linked verse", a tradition going back to the literary contests held at the imperial court of medieval Japan.

Since Bilodo found all this fascinating and felt like talking about it, he told his friend Robert about his discoveries and read him a few haiku by Bashō, Buson, and Issa, classic masters of the genre, but the delicate balance between fueki – the permanent, eternity extending beyond us – and ryuko – the fleeting, the ephemeral that passes through us – seemed to be totally lost on the clerk, who regarded it as nothing but a sophisticated form of mental masturbation. Not that he had any prejudices against Japanese literature. On the contrary: Robert pointed out that he liked manga, those popular comic strips, but especially enjoyed hentai, their erotic variants, which he warmly recommended to Bilodo, whipping out a sample to back this up.

Bilodo, eager to talk to someone more capable of sharing his intellectual enthusiasm, turned to Tania. The young waitress wasn't particularly interested at first, because it was a busy time at the Madelinot. The twinkle he had expected did appear in her eyes, though, when he spread open for her the pages of a book called Traditional Haiku of the Seventeenth Century, a valuable publication he'd borrowed from the library, which allowed the reader to marvel at haiku calligraphed in old Japanese. Tania admitted it was very beautiful and very mysterious, very mystical. Bilodo couldn't have agreed more: combining ideograms with a phonetic syllabary, the Japanese way of writing contributed to the haiku's utter density, almost succeeded in expressing the indescribable.

— ✉ —

The lovely goldfish
blowing bubbles in its bowl
swims, waving its fins

Was that poetic? Bilodo had thought at first he'd hit the bull's eye- could there be anything more Japanese than a goldfish? – but now wasn't so sure any more.

Yet he had a feeling he was on the right track, for along with "lightness, sincerity, and objectivity", "affection towards all living creatures" ranked among the haiku's noblest attributes. But didn't the subject itself leave something to be desired? With all due respect to Bill, was a fish the most appropriate animal for expressing poetry? Casting about for a more suitable creature, Bilodo thought of a bird, which already had the virtue of embodying "lightness":

Tweet-tweet goes the bird
on the antenna
with a backdrop of blue sky

Was that really any better than the fish? Bilodo, upset to be so mediocre, felt his new-found self-confidence ebbing away. Knowing theoretically what a haiku consisted of was one thing, being able to write one was quite another.

Also, the literary quality was only one aspect of the problem: regardless of their debatable artistic worth, neither the fish haiku nor the one about the bird was like a poem Grandpré might have written, and that was their basic flaw. Most important of all, he needed to write a poem that was "Grandpré-esque". Bilodo had to succeed in worming his way so snugly into the deceased's mind that Ségolène wouldn't suspect anything.

— ✉ —

It occurred to Bilodo he might do a graphological analysis of Grandpré's writings; he therefore got a book dealing with that science. He soon realised it was a discipline based on experience, an art only mastered through intensive practice, so he wondered if he'd be able to define Grandpré's personality in the short period of time available to him. In the evening, while he pored over the textbook in front of the TV, his attention was caught by comments from an actor who'd been invited to talk about his profession and explained how he'd gone about playing a famous head of state who had died a few years earlier. The performer mentioned he had begun by focusing on the great man's small gestures, his mannerisms, his ways, his habits, and had worked at copying these until eventually this process of close identification revealed to him the character's inner substance, his deepest truth. Fascinated, Bilodo closed his treatise on graphology. It struck him that what he'd just heard could be a promising lead.

At the Madelinot the next day, rather than sitting at the counter, Bilodo settled himself on the banquette Grandpré used to occupy and asked to be served what the deceased had been in the habit of ordering. Puzzled, Tania put down a tomato sandwich in front of him, which he ate while enjoying the unfamiliar view his new vantage point afforded him, not just of the restaurant but of the street beyond as well.

After lunch, while continuing his round, Bilodo carried on with the exercise by trying to imagine he was Grandpré. He closely observed the world around him, noting any incident, any detail that could give him material for a haiku. The caterpillar crawling across the pavement, for example, that openwork archway formed by intertwining tree branches overhanging the street, those squirrels bickering between the legs of a park bench, and those pink panties on a clothes line blown about by the wind – could any of it perhaps be turned into a poem?

When Bilodo reached rue des Hêtres, he leisurely strolled down the street, doing his best to see with the eyes of Grandpré, to feel what the other would have felt, and that's how it came about, when he arrived in front of the deserted apartment while trying to enter the inner world of the man who was no more, that the real way to gain access to it was suddenly revealed to him, in the form of a notice.

A red-and-black notice, sellotaped to the window, reading:

"APARTMENT FOR RENT ".

— ✉ —

Bilodo found the owner of the building in her minuscule vegetable garden. She was a well-groomed, distrustful lady who seemed to be reassured by Bilodo's uniform. Abandoning her plants momentarily, Madame Brochu took him to the third floor and let him into the apartment which, for a change, he entered quite legally this time. How strange it was to visit that place in broad daylight after he'd slunk through it in the dark. Contrary to the sinister memory he had of it, the apartment turned out to be pleasant, well lit, remarkable mainly for its typically Japanese decoration. Bilodo couldn't have been aware of it at the time of his previous intrusion – because he had only dimly seen the premises by the glow of a torch and through the glaucous prism of stress – but the furniture, the blinds, the lamps, pretty well everything was of Japanese inspiration or style. You would almost think you had been whisked away to the land of the rising sun.

Wherever Bilodo's gaze rested, it encountered the tortured shape of a bonsai, a print, a knickknack, a statuette representing a languid geisha or a shrewdly smiling podgy bonze, a touchy samurai brandishing his sword. Those padded carpets Bilodo had found it so curious to walk on were in fact tatami mats, fitted together on the floor like pieces of a gigantic puzzle. As for that thing, that peculiar object he'd knocked over as he fled, it was actually a beautiful little table made of precious wood, delicately sculpted in the shape of a leaf bending on its stem, probably used for serving tea. On either side of the writing desk, the only Western touch present, stood a tall rack stuffed with books. The living room's second area, partitioned off by a folding paper screen painted with a mountainous landscape bright with cherry trees in blossom, must have served as a dining room. All it contained was a low table, surrounded by embroidered cushions, on which sat a tiny Zen garden.

The bedroom was plainly furnished with a futon and a wardrobe whose movable panels were fitted with tall mirrors that reflected you from head to toe. As for the bathroom, it contained a curious little wooden bath, a high, narrow vat of some sort, set right inside the regular tub, to make it easier to empty no doubt.

So Grandpré had been an enthusiast of the Japanese way of life. Not at all surprising in such an ardent devotee of haiku. That outlandish scarlet dressing gown he never took off was obviously a kimono, now probably lying in some grim cupboard at the morgue, unless it had been incinerated along with its owner.

The kitchen counter was spotless, the putrid smell no longer there-Madame Brochu had seen to it. The door's broken windowpane had been replaced. Nothing hinted that the place had recently been the scene of a burglary. Somewhat flustered, Madame Brochu explained how surprised she'd been to learn that the late former tenant, who apparently had neither heirs nor close relatives, had bequeathed his furniture and all his personal belongings to her in his will. This was an inconvenience for the dear lady, who found herself forced to dispose of the articles at her own expense, but for Bilodo it represented an unexpected stroke of luck: he suggested he rent the apartment just as it was, with everything it contained – an arrangement Madame Brochu was only too happy to accept. A few minutes later Bilodo signed his lease and received the key to his new home.

Inwardly he jumped for joy, convinced he'd finally discovered how to overcome the poetic hurdle. What better way to penetrate the mystery of Grandpré's soul than by exploring his natural habitat, by living as he himself had lived? Bilodo wandered from room to room, feeling shivers of excitement racing through him before that rich deposit of existence ready to be mined. He would go through everything, immerse himself in the premises' atmosphere, breathe in their most subtle exhalation. He would vampirize the evanescent aura of the man who'd preceded him within these walls, find out everything about him, and eventually slip so deeply into his mind that he'd have no difficulty guessing, sensing, what Grandpré would have written.

Bilodo didn't discover any skeletons in Grandpré's closets or any suspicious items in his fridge, nor anything particularly noteworthy in the kitchen cupboards either, except a plentiful supply of tea and several bottles of sake. He did, however, find a phenomenal number of unmatched socks in the chest of drawers as well as in the laundry hamper, and wondered what light this odorous enigma shed on the deceased's psychology. Did Grandpré steal socks from laundromats? Did he collect them? Did he turn into a centipede when the moon was full? Otherwise, the apartment contained nothing out of the ordinary.

What impressed Bilodo most was the sheer number of books on the shelves. The majority were by Japanese authors, of course. Hundreds of volumes were lined up there, bearing exotic titles and names. He opened at random a novel by a certain Mishima and came across a passage where a young woman squeezed a little mother's milk from her breast, which she then put into her lover's tea. Disturbed by such a strange gesture, Bilodo closed the book again and, deciding to complete his literary education at a later date, began to study those of Grandpré's papers that he hadn't been able to take with him the night of the break-in.

That's how he discovered a letter from Ségolène, a conventional one, entirely in prose, dating back three years. Writing to Grandpré for the first time, the Guadeloupean woman introduced herself as a lover of Japanese poetry and commented favourably on an article by Grandpré about the art of haiku according to Kobayashi Issa that had appeared in a journal of literary studies. Other letters followed. They showed how quickly an intellectual closeness had developed between them and how after a while the renku project was born – an idea of Grandpré's. So this was the way they became acquainted. A shared interest in Japanese literature had caused them to cross paths and strike up a friendship. At least one mystery had been cleared up.

Encouraged by this first breakthrough, Bilodo decided to take another stab at writing poetry. He had a whole weekend, since it was Friday, so he locked the door, closed the blinds, and invoked the old masters, respectfully requesting their benevolence. Then, like someone fishing for pearl oysters, he dived into his inner self.

Because Bilodo believed his previous haiku suffered from a lack of fueki – the eternity element – he spent all night writing a poem he meant to be a celebration of the dazzling return of dawn, finishing it in the small hours:

The sun rises, climbs
on the horizon
like a big, golden balloon

It wasn't too bad, Bilodo felt. It had plenty of fueki anyway. But wasn't the ryuko content – the ephemeral or mundane element – insufficient, though? What Bilodo was aiming for was the delicate balance that characterized a good haiku, so he set to work again, making every effort to proportion these two contradictory constituents correctly.

The sun is rising –
I put cheese slices
on my buttered toast

The sun is rising
like a big, golden navel
on an empty gut

The sun is rising

like a golden cheese —

now let's go and have breakfast.

Bilodo noticed his stomach grumbled. Not surprising, considering he hadn't eaten anything since the day before, wrapped up as he'd been in his creative endeavour. Did one thing explain another, he wondered? Was poetry basically an affair of the stomach after all? Bilodo put the question on hold and went to have lunch at the Délicieux Orient, a local Japanese restaurant.

— ✉ —

In the late afternoon he had a visit from Madame Brochu, who brought a fruit basket as a welcome gift. The lady noted the progress he'd made in settling in and insisted on making sure he had everything he needed. Grasping the opportunity to find out more about Grandpré, Bilodo invited her to stay for tea and served it on the pretty little leaf-shaped table. After they'd traded the usual polite remarks, Bilodo steered the conversation onto the former tenant. The dreadful circumstances of his death were recalled, commented on, deplored. Bilodo learned Grandpré had taught literature at the College nearby, but had retired the previous year although he was still quite young. Drawn out by Bilodo's keen attention, the lady revealed the poor man had behaved strangely in the last months of his life —

he hardly ever left his apartment and played the same recordings of Chinese music over and over. A breakdown of some kind, she assumed, just barely able to bring herself to whisper that word of doom.

After Madame Brochu left, Bilodo drained the teapot while thinking things over. In many respects his knowledge of Grandpré's personality remained hazy, and the intricacies of his mind largely unexplored, but Bilodo was beginning to see daylight. The lady's account had added a new element: music. Would it contribute, Bilodo wondered, to a better understanding of the man? As soon as he started rummaging through Grandpré's discs, he found the recordings of Chinese music the lady had mentioned – it was traditional Japanese music, actually. He chose one at random and put it on. The pleasing tones of a melancholy flute and chords plucked from a kind of lute filtered from the speakers, pervading the living room with a sweet recitative. Inspired all of a sudden, Bilodo grabbed his pen...

— ✉ —

He wrote, putting on disc after disc, guzzling tea, while the shadowy hours slipped by. Arpeggios rippled from the koto, sometimes accompanied by a shrillish samisen, sometimes a sho, emphasizing the ethereal tone of a hichiriki or spellbinding nasal singing of a woman. Bilodo wrote as if in a trance, striving with his whole being towards wabi (sober beauty in harmony with nature), immersing himself in the age-old virtues of sabi (simplicity, serenity, solitude). He took an imaginary stroll through the autumnal blaze of Mount Royal and tried to render the contagious languor of the shameless trees, the rustle of leaves startled by the wind, the song of birds about to depart, and the last crunchings of insects.

He wrote, seeking the words' cooperation, struggling to seize them in midair before they scattered, to capture them like butterflies in the page's net and pin them to the paper. Every so often he achieved a line he considered tolerably good, only to decide five minutes later it rang hollow and feed it to the wastepaper basket. He'd start over, wading in a pond of crumpled cellulose, taking an occasional break to draw a hieroglyph in the sand of the tiny Zen garden or reread a certain haiku by Grandpré or Ségolène, reciting them out loud the better to admire their resonant spontaneity.

He had sushi delivered by the Délicieux Orient, which he took care to eat when Bill wasn't looking, then continued all night covering the snowy white paper with his scribbles, and all day Sunday, living on sake now, and again all evening, until his head spun, he'd developed a squint, and the pen fell from his fingers. He flopped down on the futon and sank into a sleep haunted by living ideograms and dreamt that Ségolène opened her blouse and squeezed a little milk from her breast, which she let drip between his own lips...

When he woke up on Monday morning with his neurons in a jumble, he swallowed four aspirins, took an interminable shower, then

sorted through the few sheets that deserved to escape destruction and
ended up choosing a poem written at twilight:

The sun is setting –
it yawns on the balcony
snores at my window

The tercet gave off a whiff of poetry, Bilodo thought, and didn't
strike him as totally foreign to what Grandpé might have written.
It was almost right. But almost wasn't quite enough yet, and he
methodically tore the sheet into infinitesimal pieces he sent whirling
about like snowflakes. For the second time in two weeks he called the
Post Office to say he wouldn't be coming in to work, then heated water
for his tea and started slogging away again, determined to sacrifice an
entire forest if he had to.

It was almost noon when the banging of the letterbox made him
jump. Bilodo noted with a slight pang of jealousy that replacing him
didn't appear to have been much of a problem and went to pick up
Grandpré's post. There were two advertising flyers, one bill, and a
letter from Ségolène.

— ✉ —

It took Bilodo a moment to get a grip on himself. This was totally
unexpected. He never thought Ségolène would write before Grandpré

had replied to her haiku about the baby otter. With the paper knife in his trembling hand, he slit open the envelope. It contained as always only a single sheet: .

Have I displeased you?
Forget the autumn
do I still have your friendship?

Bilodo felt strongly challenged by the haiku's frank, direct tone and was alarmed by the almost palpable anxiety it conveyed. Used to more punctuality from her penfriend, Ségolène obviously worried about his silence; the poor woman was afraid she had offended him in some way. Bilodo imagined her uneasiness as she wrote the poem, anxiety spreading over her lovely face, attacking its sweet fullness. That vision of Ségolène falling prey to anguish was more than he could bear, and he felt an urgent need to act. He needed to reply very quickly to reassure her and bring back her smile. Bilodo must stop dragging his feet and finally deliver that blasted haiku!

The grass barely filled the gaps on Gaston Grandpré's freshly sodded grave. Bilodo sank into a meditative state. Hoping to stir what was left of the deceased, perhaps his lingering soul, he silently depicted Ségolène's anxiety, the urgent nature of the situation, and stressed that his intentions were honest, his feelings sincere. Most humbly he told the man slumbering underground of his diligent efforts to imitate his works, and begged him respectfully to enlighten him: what could he do? Was there some action yet to be taken, some sacrifice he needed to agree to, some key he might have failed to insert into the complicated lock of the door barring his way to poetry?

Kneeling on the damp grass, Bilodo waited, listened with every fibre of his being, but not a single revelation issued from the grave, no sepulchral voice burst forth. Apparently the deceased had no advice to communicate. And yet...

— ✉ —

As though in response to his visit to the cemetery, Bilodo dreamt about Grandpré that night. He dreamt in fact that he woke up and found Grandpré at his bedside, wrapped in his red kimono. The ghost was smiling in spite of the blood spattered on his pale brow, his tangled hair. His smile never fading, he moved through the room as though rolling on ball bearings. He went up to the wardrobe in this way, opened its door, and pointed at the top shelf...

Bilodo woke up in earnest. Theoretically at least. Could this be just a fractal of a deeper dream, he wondered – was he only dreaming that he had woken up – or was it real this time? Then he noticed there was no ghostly Grandpré anywhere in sight and opted for the second eventuality. He looked at the wardrobe, puzzling over the gesture the ghost had made to direct him towards the shelf. It had been just a dream, of course, but Bilodo's curiosity got the better of him and he decided to go and take a closer look, just in case. He opened the wardrobe. The top shelf was high and deep. Bilodo stretched out his hand, explored the cavity with his fingertips. He touched something. A box stowed away at the very back. Startled, he pulled it towards him. It was a black cardboard box, quite large, not very heavy, printed with Japanese ideograms. Bilodo put it on the bed and lifted the lid.

Folded in thin tissue paper was a red kimono.

$$- \enspace \boxtimes \enspace -$$

The kimono didn't look as if it had ever been worn. Bilodo took it out of the box, unfolded it. The fabric was silky, iridescent. A truly beautiful garment. Bilodo couldn't resist putting it on. To his amazement he felt perfectly comfortable in it. He took a few steps and spun around and around to see how light the kimono was. He sent the flaps flying about him – he felt a bit like Lawrence of Arabia in his first emir costume – and admired himself in the mirror. The garment moulded itself completely to his body. It looked as though it were made for him. Bilodo felt electric. It was as if a mild current flowed through his nerves, causing him to tingle all over. On a sudden impulse he left the bedroom, headed into the living room, sat down at the desk, put a blank sheet of paper in front of him, picked up a pen, placed its point on the paper. Then the miracle happened. The tip of the ballpoint started rolling over the sheet, inscribed it with a seismographic string of words. Could Bilodo still be dreaming? Inspiration had suddenly struck. It was like a dam giving way inside him, like a stalled engine finally starting. He could barely keep up with the images as they crowded into his consciousness, knocked against one another like billiard balls.

A minute later, it was finished: the mysterious force had abandoned Bilodo, leaving him haggard, worn out. Before him lay a haiku. It had written itself, in one go, without a single deletion, automatically, in handwriting one would have sworn was Grandpré's:

Perpetual snow
on lofty heights, unchanging
such is my friendship

Bilodo tried to make sense of what just happened; he thought it might be a conditioning phenomenon of some kind, the catalyst of which had been the discovery of the kimono. Putting on the garment, slipping symbolically into Grandpré's skin had probably triggered the creative process he'd been trying to start for days. Or was it spiritualism? Had Bilodo been briefly possessed? Had Grandpré's spirit granted his wish so as to help him? Bilodo felt too shaken to decide. The important thing was the poem: whether under spiritual influence or not, Bilodo had just written what he thought was the first good haiku of his life. Would it succeed, though, in comforting Ségolène? Would it appeal to her?

Bilodo folded the paper and slipped it into an envelope. But just as he was about to close it, he hesitated, tormented by one last dilemma: should he add that stylized O to the haiku – the one Grandpré used to draw on everything? Was it some kind of signature or graphic seal, the absence of which might arouse suspicion? To find out, he would have needed to examine the deceased's previous mailings; once again the loss of Grandpré's last letter made itself sorely felt. Bilodo finally chanced forgoing it. He sealed the envelope and hurried to post it before he changed his mind.

It would take five or six days for the haiku to reach Ségolène and at least as many for her reply to get back to him – supposing that she replied, that she didn't suspect the deception, that the ruse worked.

— ✉ —

The letter arrived eleven days later. Bilodo had been hoping for it with all the passion he had inside him, praying for it constantly, no longer daring to touch his pen or put on the kimono for fear of jeopardizing fate's delicate balance, but there it was at last, in his hand, as he stood transfixed at his counter in the Depot. Unable to wait, he rushed to the men's room, locked himself in the last cubicle, tore open the envelope, and read:

Sheer, towering peaks
respectful regards from your
humble mountaineer

Bilodo was instantly transported into a Himalayan landscape worthy of Tintin in Tibet. Clinging to a rock, he stood halfway up a steep, downhill slope of virgin snow, dazzling in the harsh sunlight, while ahead of him rose the summit, far off and yet close by in the

~197~

rarefied air, sharply outlined against the deep blue sky, moody, imperious in its rugged grandeur...

When after all that time Bilodo finally savoured Ségolène's words again, he felt invigorated, strong as a yeti. It was like a transfusion after a haemorrhage, a puff of oxygen when you are suffocating. He jubilated in the washroom. It had worked! She had believed in it!

Some austere mountains
secretly hope that at last
someone dare climb them

They act tough, flaunting
their avalanche clothes
but they are tender-hearted

They are scared at night
weep with loneliness
their tears create waterfalls

This is how mountain
lakes pool into existence
in icy silence

— ✉ —

Bilodo felt his happiness was complete. What more could he want? The kimono hung waiting for him in the wardrobe, but he was careful not to use it too often; he saved it, donned it only when it was time to reply to Ségolène. Then all he needed to do was put the miraculous garment on and his soul took wing, whizzed away, while colours and visions came rushing in. Bilodo had finally rejected any kind of supernatural explanation for the phenomenon. He reckoned that his discovery of the kimono right after the dream about a ghostly Grandpré was simply a fortunate coincidence, and as for the rest, that was just the subconscious manifesting itself. Besides, he didn't really want to delve more deeply into the issue, because he feared that being too inquisitive might slow down his creative momentum and jeopardize the poetry. The basic cause of the miracle wasn't particularly important to him, as long as it worked and he could keep writing to Ségolène, as long as he could dream about her playing the flute on the bank of the lazy river, charming snakes as in that painting by Henri Rousseau, then dozing on a bed of greenery while wildflowers wrapped her in live petals and forest animals mounted a jealous guard by her side.

Shimmering forms – dawn
through half-closed lashes
iridescent theatre

A flower flies from
the hair of the fruit vendor
it's a butterfly

Mini-monster commandos
haunting the pavements
on Halloween night

A runaway horse
he looks terrified!
what's biting him, I wonder?

Crystal-glazed puddles
the grass crunches underfoot
another winter

My big cat purrs on the bed –
right under his nose
the mouse scampers off

The perfect beauty
the divine architecture
of a soft snowflake

Enormous black backs
whip up the ocean –
the sperm whales are frolicking

— ✉ —

She swam and gambolled, enormous, yet so nimble. Her dark, streamlined body undulated gracefully, stood out against the sunlight on the shimmering screen of the surface, skimming the sparkling curtain, sometimes cleaving it with her back. She swam and melodized, she filled the ocean with her songs, because she was a whale. And so was he. They were whales and swam together, they were heading over yonder, to that place that had no name, that was simply "over yonder", far off in the infinite blue expanse. They were in no hurry. They dawdled, glided in a muted twilight glow. They would hunt a little, then let themselves be carried along, trusting the currents. They'd come up now and again to blow out a geyser of iodized steam and fill their lungs with air, to drift for a spell, swaying gently with the waves, then they'd go down again to where it was calm.

It was good to be a whale. It was good to be with her, just with her, and be free together. If he had had a choice, he would rather have been the ocean so he could have hugged Ségolène even more closely, and put his endless water arms around her everywhere at once, and slid all over her skin forever, but even so it was nice to be a whale. It was a great joy, as long as she was there and together they could escape time.

Now she sounded all of a sudden. She went into a nosedive, fled from the light. Had she detected an appetizing prey? Was it just for the fun of getting to the bottom of things, of exploring some unfamiliar wreck, or was she playing hide-and-seek? He followed her, plunging with powerful strokes of his tail; he wasn't going to lag behind. He dived after her to where the darkness deepened, surrounded you, held you in an ever tighter, ever colder grip. He had already lost sight of her but could feel the vibrations of the mass of water she displaced, and he heard her sing in the gloom close by. She was calling. She was calling him, and he answered, also with a song, because that was how you communicated when you were a whale – you sang into the void, unafraid of the darkness that grew ever darker, ever deeper.

A kid is shouting

he's waving his stick about

he just scored a goal

The little girl screams

On the window ledge

she has seen a centipede

On the clothes line in the yard

the washing freezes

and sparrows shiver

My neighbour Aimée
gardens in a floral dress
You would water her

— ✉ —

January was wreaking its havoc. It had already been three
months since Bilodo moved into Grandpré's place. He now felt
perfectly at home there but continued to think "at Grandpré's place".
It was automatic, but also a mark of respect for the man to whom he
owed so much happiness. He only went over to his old apartment
when it suited him, to pick up his scanty post and delete from his
voicemail the smutty propositions that kept flooding into it. His
furniture and most of his things were still there. He had hardly moved
anything into Grandpré's place, not wanting to alter its pleasing
Oriental atmosphere. He could have sublet his old apartment now that
he didn't need it any more, but had decided not to, because he used
that official address as both a cover and an alibi so as to preserve the
tranquillity of the parallel life he led in his lair on rue des Hêtres. That
way, he didn't have to fear either visits from unwelcome guests or ill-
timed intrusions by Robert. Bilodo hadn't told the clerk anything, and
the mere thought of him turning up with his huge clogs in the muffled
seclusion of his Japanese sanctuary made him shudder. Robert, who
was no fool, suspected something, of course. It struck him as odd
that Bilodo never answered the phone and was never home when

he stopped by. Robert's questions were becoming embarrassing and Bilodo found it more and more difficult to evade them.

Apart from Robert's nosy queries, the outside world rarely intervened in Bilodo's cloistered life, centred completely on his imaginary romance. There was Tania, at the Madelinot, who never missed an opportunity to gab and ask how his research into Japanese poetry was coming along. As a matter of fact, Bilodo had got into the habit of devoting his lunch break, after dessert, to the revision of haiku he meant to send to Ségolène, and Tania, puzzled, often asked him what he was writing and if she could read it. He refused as nicely as possible, on the pretext that it was too personal, but the young waitress continued to show a keen interest in his writings, which was rather touching. He was sorry he always had to say no to Tania. And because he wanted her to like him, he promised he'd write a haiku especially for her one day. She seemed thrilled.

Apart from that, Bilodo saw practically no one. There was Madame Brochu, with whom he exchanged the occasional polite remark, although more briefly since a recent incident: when she came knocking at his door to ask him to turn down the volume of his Chinese music, the lady had looked shocked at seeing him wearing Grandpré's kimono. She had been less cordial after that and eyed Bilodo suspiciously ever since. It was understandable, he thought. Judged from the outside, his behaviour was certainly surprising. Judged from the inside as well: living the way he did, having slipped into someone else's mind and clothing, surely denoted a high degree of eccentricity. But he fully accepted being odd in this respect, no matter what other people might think. The important point was never to lose sight of the deeper logic.

— ✉ —

A wandering man
found frozen to death
on a bench, today at dawn

La Soufrière – its
head in the clouds as though in
elevated thoughts

It's been snowing hard
thirty centimetres now
snow-blower heaven

Vidé touloulou
It's the Grand brilé Vaval
ti-punch flows freely

= ✉ =

Vidé, in Creole, was a parade, a procession, because in Guade loupe, too, it was the end of February, carnival time. Touloulou was a dance for which the ladies enjoyed the privilege of choosing their partners, while Vaval was the king of the festival, the local mascot, sort of the Bonhomme Carnaval of the area. The Grand brilé was a popular ceremony that took place on the evening of Ash Wednesday and concluded the carnival with the burning of the unfortunate Vaval amid cries and wails from the hysterical crowd. As for the freely flowing ti-punch, that was clear enough. Bilodo supposed it was probably all very much like the Quebec Carnival, but fifty degrees warmer.

Eager to share Ségolène's festive mood and show her that celebrations around here were every bit as joyful as the ones on her island, he sent her a rousing:

Swing your partner round and round
gents fall back one and
swing the girl behind!

And he, who had never set as much as a toe on a dance floor, dreamt that night that he whirled around merrily with Ségolène in the unlikely, highly diverse setting of a festive town that was a cross between Vieux-Québec and Pointe-à-Pitre. He dreamt that they danced now a frenzied rigadoon on the icy pavement of Place d'

Youville, now a wild gwoka in the fragrant sultriness of Place de la Victoire. And Ségolène laughed and twirled around, never tiring, her hair whipping the night.

······· ·······
13
······· ·······

On the first Monday in March a parcel arrived from France, addressed to Gaston Grandpré. It contained a manuscript called Enso, which was written by Grandpré himself and had an illustration of a black circle with a frayed outline on the cover page. That mysterious circle again, the O that showed up on all of the deceased's papers.

With the document came a short letter from the editor of a free-form poetry series published by Éditions du Roseau in Paris. The editor acknowledged the work had certain good qualities, but he regretted he was unable to accept it for publication. Bilodo leafed through the manuscript, a mere sixty or so pages, each containing a single haiku. He wasn't really surprised to discover that the opening poem of the collection was well known to him:

Swirling like water
against rugged rocks
time goes around and around

The following haiku were familiar to him as well: he had read
them many times, sometimes in versions somewhat dissimilar to
those he now had before him:

They come from the east
gulls screeching like witches at
a midnight revel

A steep granite spine
wild tangle of spruce
and then at long last the beach

Magnificent sweep
Oh! the utter perfection
of that golfer's swing

His driver of light
sending the ball soaring high
up among the stars

Having only dipped into Grandpré's haiku in a random fashion until now – perusing a poem here and there among the man's chaotic papers – Bilodo found it to be a very different experience to read them in the particular order in which the author had placed them. Their specific sequence gave them a kind of incantatory power. As Bilodo turned the manuscript's pages, he had the impression he was heading towards a hidden goal, that he moved in spite of himself towards an implacable fate. The haiku resonated against one another, producing a music of the mind with a haunting rhythm. They gave him an archetypal sensation of déjà vu, of having experienced or, rather, dreamt it all before. They stirred up old images in deep strata of his memory.

In the ocean depths
gloom is a meaningless word
down there the light kills

Ribcage perfectly
picked clean, the march of
necrophagous centuries

To break through the horizon
look behind the set
meet and embrace Death

Rejoice, mermaids and mermen
the Prince of the Deep
has returned to you.

Dark and yet luminous, the haiku followed one another, a procession of pelagic fish exuding their own phosphorescence. The collection's title puzzled Bilodo; he looked up the word Enso in the dictionary but couldn't find it. Falling back on the Internet, he had the satisfaction of seeing many references displayed on the screen, all showing circles similar to the one on the cover page, and discovered this to be a traditional symbol in Zen Buddhism. The Enso circle represented the emptiness of the mind allowing one to attain enlightenment (satori). Having been painted by Zen masters for thousands of years, it prompted a spiritual exercise in meditation on nothingness. The circle, drawn with a single continuous brushstroke – without hesitating, without thinking – was believed to reveal the artist's state of mind: one could only trace a powerful, well-balanced Enso when one's mind was clear, free of all thought or intention.

As he tried to find out more, Bilodo learnt that the Zen circle could be interpreted in numerous ways: it could represent just as well perfection, truth, or infinity, simplicity, the cycle of the seasons, or the turning wheel. On the whole, Enso symbolized the loop, the cyclical nature of the universe, history always repeating itself, the perpetual return to the starting point. It was similar in that sense to the Greek

Ouroboros symbol, depicting a serpent biting its own tail.

Enso, a rich and diverse symbol, and a title that took on its full, definitive meaning when one reached the manuscript's last page, which contained the same haiku as the collection's first page:

Swirling like water
against rugged rocks
time goes around and around

The repetition couldn't possibly be accidental. Grandpré had meant it this way; he had given his collection the shape of a loop. The return to the opening poem, which itself evoked the loop, was Enso, the Zen circle, the book perpetually repeating itself.

Lost in thought, Bilodo closed the manuscript. He regretted it had been rejected by the publisher. The work brought together Grandpré's best poems, his most accomplished ones, and it being turned down like this seemed unfair: the guys at that publishing house were obviously asleep at the wheel. But they weren't the only publishers in the world after all. Checking the Web once more, Bilodo got a list of the leading publishers of Quebec poetry and made a decision: he was going to submit the manuscript elsewhere. Someone somewhere was sure to see the light.

He would get the collection published. It was a posthumous duty he felt entrusted with. Wasn't it the least he could do to honour the memory of Grandpré – the pioneer who had blazed a trail for him that led to Ségolène?

On the canoe floor
a suffocating trunkfish
drowning in the air

Being a frog and
breathing through the skin
truly the best of both worlds

Raindrop on the leaf
for a ladybug
a natural disaster

The faithful master
leans over and scoops
who is really on the leash?

La Désirade's waves
clear and luminous
like a tanka by Bashō

— ✉ —

Bilodo had grown somewhat familiar with Bashō that fine haiku poet of the seventeenth century, but just what was a tanka again? He knew the word. He remembered coming across it during his literary explorations the previous autumn.

It didn't take him long to track it down in Grandpré's books. The tanka was the oldest, most elevated classical Japanese verse form; its art had been practised exclusively at the Imperial Court. It was the haiku's ancestor, the venerable forefather the haiku descended from. It was a more extensive poem, having five lines rather than three, and consisted of two parts: the first one, a tercet of seventeen syllables, was simply that good old haiku, while the second, an added-on distich made up of two lines of seven syllables each, responded in some way to the first and gave the stanza a new direction. Bilodo learnt that either form had its own, particular subject area. Unlike the haiku – a brief poem speaking to the senses and tending to involve the observation of nature – the tanka was meant to be lyrical, exquisite, refined. Its practitioners strove to explore noble themes and sentiments such as love, loneliness, death. The poem was devoted to the expression of complex emotions.

Bilodo shivered. What did that allusion by Ségolène to the tanka mean? Was it a subtle message, an invitation?

A form favouring the expression of feelings. Wasn't that precisely what Bilodo longed for? Hadn't he felt constricted at times by the limitations the haiku imposed on him? Wasn't he tired, quite frankly, of evoking weather reports, clothes lines, and little birds? Hadn't the time come to contemplate grander, more beautiful things and break out of the tight, binding garment? Didn't he feel the desire to go further, to finally lay bare his heart?

Bilodo slipped on his kimono, then started writing, eager to experiment with the unfamiliar form, and was surprised to find he had no trouble coming to grips with it. The stanza materialized all by itself, dropped into his hands like a ripe fruit:

Some flowers, it seems
take seven years to open
For a long, long time
I have wanted to tell you
how intensely I love you

Proud of his first tanka, euphoric, Bilodo rushed out to post it. It wasn't until later, once his adrenalin level had gone back to normal, that he began to reflect on what he'd done and doubt crept into his mind.

— ✉ —

Was it wise – if you really thought about it – to send Ségolène a poem so different from the ones she usually received? It wasn't the form he worried about but the content: how would the young woman react to the explicit declaration, this sudden intrusion in the formerly reserved sphere of feelings? Might it not alienate her? Would the sweet, subtle bond between them not suffer by it? Hadn't Bilodo been too bold?

He now regretted acting so impetuously, but the harm was done: the tanka lay at the bottom of the postbox on the other side of the street, irretrievable. In theory, at least. Wasn't Robert, whose duties included collecting the post, supposed to show up towards noon?

Not long before that time, Bilodo went out to wait for Robert, walking up and down past the postbox like a neurotic sentry, deaf to the warbling of birds another April brought back from the south. Finally, after half an hour, the van appeared. It drew up alongside the pavement and Robert got out with loud whoops of delight at finding his old pal Libido there. Cutting the outpouring short, Bilodo explained the favour he expected from his friend. Robert appeared reluctant at first, arguing that what Bilodo asked of him was highly irregular, but it was just to keep him in suspense for a bit – how much weight did a few stupid regulations really carry compared with the unbreakable brotherly bond uniting them?

Once he'd relieved the postbox of its contents, the postal clerk had Bilodo get into the van with him, and there, safe from the rabble's prying eyes, he emptied his bag, invited Bilodo to fish out that famous letter he said he'd posted by mistake. While mumbling incoherently from sheer gratitude, Bilodo spread about the various parcels, envelopes, used syringes, stolen hockey jumpers, and other vile things the box had excreted, and found his letter. All danger was passed now, and Bilodo felt relieved, although vaguely disappointed, without quite knowing why. Robert's snooping eyes had nevertheless deciphered the address on the envelope. Since the clerk hadn't believed Bilodo's lame excuse for a minute and sensed there might be a woman behind all this, he demanded to know who that Ségolène was Bilodo was writing to in Guadeloupe. Bilodo instinctively concealed the letter in his jacket. Grateful as he might be to Robert, he refused to talk, stated it was strictly confidential. Contrary to expectation, Robert didn't push the matter, but warned his friend he wouldn't be let off the hook without at least going for a drink with him after work, to celebrate. Bilodo hesitated, knowing how easily an invitation of this sort could lead to things getting out of control, but after what Robert had just done for him, how could he refuse?

······ ······
15
······ ······

Bilodo dreamt he heard someone laughing. As he woke up, it took him a minute to realise he was lying fully dressed on the futon with the blinds open and the morning sun stamped right onto his face. He tried to get up, then abandoned the idea, floored by a throbbing ache boring into his skull. The memory of last night's excesses came back to him in snatches. There was that pub on rue Ontario where the night out began, those glasses of Scotch appearing one after the other at the bar. What came next was already a bit blurred: there was that club with female dancers on the rue Stanley, also a cubicle where sensual beauties swayed their hips in close-up, then the massage parlour Robert had dragged him off to against his will, then that Hawaiian pizza ingested on a banquette in a glaringly bright restaurant, then yet another place – a bar? a club? – but he had absolutely no recollection of what came after.

And there were those questions. Those indiscreet questions from Robert who quizzed him again and again about the letter, about Ségolène, and relentlessly returned to the charge as the night wore on, as things got more and more out of hand. The clerk had obviously meant to take advantage of his alcoholic stupor to get the full lowdown. What had Bilodo let slip? He had to admit he had no idea. What did he tell Robert? What had happened during those black bits that hatched the mental film of the night?

The laugh he'd heard in his dream rang out again, except that Bilodo was wide awake this time. It came from the next room. Someone was laughing in the living room. With a shock Bilodo recognised Robert's distinctive braying and realised the clerk was right there, in the adjoining room. A squirt of fresh memory data splashed onto his mind: he suddenly remembered that after the wild spree, in the small hours of the morning, he had stupidly let his friend drive him home. His new home! His secret refuge!

He recalled Robert's drunken amazement when he found out the little sneak had moved without telling anyone, and then his surprise when he discovered the Japanese décor of Bilodo's new lair. He recalled how his friend had explored the premises, looking for a geisha, drained a bottle of sake, pissed in the bathtub, knocked over the little tea table, then collapsed on the tatami and snored like a B-52 in search of a city to drop an atom bomb on. Bilodo's migraine flared up. What an unforgivable blunder! Now the secret of his private fortress was out. Robert knew. He was right there, in the living room, and he was laughing. What could he be finding so funny?

Bilodo managed to get up in spite of his seasickness and navigated his way into the corridor. Another burst of laughter from Robert. Bilodo held on to the wall and reached the doorway to the living room, where he found Robert in his boxer shorts and undershirt slouched in the armchair at the desk. He was reading something he obviously thought highly comical. And that thing was a haiku by Ségolène.

The drawer was open. The young woman's poems were scattered about on the desk and Robert had a few of them in his hand, defiling them with his sacrilegious gaze while he scratched his scrotum and even had the gall to recite them in his croaking Pithecanthropus voice.

"They act tough, flaunting / their avalanche clothes / but they are tender-hearted," Robert said, guffawing. "In those clothes I guess they'd call a blow job a snow job."

At the sight of the clerk in his underwear holding Ségolène's refined poems between his fat, disgusting fingers, sullying them with his glowering stare and coarse laugh, Bilodo felt his blood turning to ice in his veins. In the toneless voice of a robot about to break the First Law, he ordered Robert to give the sheets back to him, but Robert seemed in no hurry to comply.

"Wait," he said, flipping through the poems, "The other ones are even lousier."

And the clerk did it again, read another haiku in a ridiculous falsetto voice. Bilodo moved towards him. Robert had expected that. He jumped out of the chair and ran to the other end of the room. Bilodo pursued him, determined to get the precious poems back no matter what. He finally outwitted the miserable clown's manoeuvrings and managed to catch hold of them, but that idiot wouldn't let go, so the inevitable happened... Bilodo stared, bewildered, at the fragments of the torn sheets Robert still clutched, and then at the ones in his own hand.

"Oops!" said Robert, roaring with laughter.

"Get out." Bilodo ordered in a monotone.

"Relax," the clerk shot back defiantly, "Let's not get all worked up about three or four shitty poems!"

Did he really say "shitty"? As swiftly as it had solidified, Bilodo's blood liquefied, instantly reaching the boiling point. His fist clenched, lashed out, punched Robert on the nose. The clerk was hurled through the cherry trees on the folding screen and crashed down on the low table behind it. Bilodo snatched the shreds of paper from between his fingers. Dazed, holding his bloody nose, the clerk picked himself up as best he could and had the nerve to take it badly. He swore, flailed his arms, tried to strike back, but his blow only grazed his co-worker's ear. Bilodo retaliated by planting a hefty right in his belly. Robert deflated, all the aggressiveness draining out of him along with the air in his lungs. Bilodo took advantage of it to pick him up by his vest, and dragged him to the hallway, just barely taking time to open the door before heaving him out. Robert, flung out onto the staircase, bounced down three steps on his backside. Bilodo threw his clothes at him and bolted the door.

He couldn't believe it. He who had never hurt a fly without regretting that he couldn't give it an anaesthetic first had just hit his best friend. His ex-friend, that is. But he had a more pressing concern right now. It was a serious moment: some of Ségolène's loveliest haiku were in shreds. Indifferent to the insults and dire warnings Robert was uttering outside, as well as his violent banging on the door, Bilodo got out a roll of sellotape and applied himself to piecing the treasured sheets together again. Behind the door Robert had begun to make threats, swearing he wasn't going to get away with it, he'd get his own back sooner or later, but Bilodo didn't hear a thing, engrossed as he was in the delicate surgical operation of mending the mutilated verse.

It wasn't until later – long after Robert's shouts had died away, once Ségolène's poetry had been fully restored – that Bilodo realised, as he searched in his jacket pocket for the unsent letter he'd slipped into it the previous day, that it wasn't there any more. It had vanished along with the tanka it contained.

He had no recollection of what he might have done with it. Had he foolishly mislaid it during last night's cavorting, or had that scumbag Robert swiped it?

When Bilodo walked into the Madelinot at lunchtime, he noticed
Robert sitting with the inevitable band of colleagues in the postal
workers' spot. The swelling and abnormal hues of his nose were
hard to miss. Bilodo felt a volley of hostile looks focusing on him;
Robert had obviously circulated a highly biased version of the nasal
attack. Bilodo tried to ignore the prevailing animosity. He took a seat
at the counter. Tania came over to put a bowl of soup down before
him and, as he began spooning it up, he pondered how to tackle the
tricky business of the filched tanka. Did Robert actually have it in his
possession? Putting the question to him point-blank was unthinkable,
especially in front of the others. How could he find out, he wondered,
without compromising himself, or running the risk the clerk might

somehow take advantage of the situation? And, should it be necessary, how could he get the letter back without being forced to eat humble pie and apologise to him, or even worse, depending on how foul his mood was? Bilodo absently chewed his shepherd's pie, hoping Robert would clarify things himself by coming over and naming the amount of the ransom, but it didn't happen: there was nothing in the clerk's attitude that led one to believe he might have any other intention towards Bilodo than to hate him until the end of time.

After lunch, as he stepped out of the men's toilets, he almost collided with Tania, who stood right there, beside the door, waiting for him. Beaming, the young woman said she wanted to thank him. For the poem, of course. And Bilodo saw she had a sheet of paper in her hand. The tanka!

Her eyes moist with happiness, Tania explained how pleasantly surprised she'd been to find the poem on the counter, along with the bill and the money owing. She confessed she was deeply touched by it, and modestly lowered her gaze before adding with a blush that she felt the same way. Bilodo, dumbfounded, finally understood: she thought the tanka was for her, that he'd written it for her as promised, and that... This was so horrific it took his breath away. He couldn't string two coherent words together, and even less shatter Tania's illusions; all he could manage was an inane smile. The young woman, who must have put his confusion down to shyness, was tactful enough to drop the subject, and merely looked at him one last time with shining eyes before going back to work.

Bilodo breathed again. The situation hadn't only overtaken him —
it now had a one-lap lead. No need to look too far for the perpetrator
of this vile plot: down at the other end of the restaurant, Robert's
fiendish smile was explanation enough. How the son of a bitch
gloated over his revenge! Bilodo grabbed his jacket and slipped out,
but not without answering Tania's little wave full of thrilling hidden
meanings. Enraged, he went to wait for Robert near his van.

The clerk showed up ten minutes later. Still sporting that
jubilant grin that was his odious speciality, Robert asked when the
wedding would be. Bilodo bristled with anger as he reproached him
for deceitfully involving Tania in a disagreement that concerned only
them. Robert sardonically assured him he'd just wanted to make
Tania happy, although he'd never understood why she was so crazy
about a stupid bastard like him. Stupid, yes, Bilodo agreed he really
must be pretty dense for not having noticed sooner what a filthy pig
Robert was. The clerk snapped back that was still better than being
a moronic asshole and warned Bilodo he had seen nothing yet, from
now on it was open war between them. Following which he took off
like a shot.

Because Bilodo knew from having seen Robert in action how
implacable he could be when he wanted to, he spent the rest of the
day worrying about the various forms, each one more harrowing than

the next, his threats were likely to take. With respect to Tania in any case, one thing was certain: no matter how disappointing this might be for her, he had to tell her the truth.

— ✉ —

Robert's threats didn't take long to materialize. When Bilodo arrived at the Depot the next day, he spotted with utter dismay on the staff lounge notice board a photocopy of his tanka carrying his forged signature; it had been printed on pink paper for greater visual impact. Other copies had been distributed all through the centre, particularly in the sorting cubicles, from which peals of laughter rang out. The whole world seemed to have read his poem. It was the joke of the day: anyone running into Bilodo put in their two cents' worth with some little allusion to love, to flowers, or to horticulture in general. Since there was nothing to be done about it, the postman took refuge in an aloof silence, stoically enduring the snub. When he could finally leave for his round, it felt like a release, but a fast three-hour walk was barely long enough to settle his nerves.

Shortly before noon Bilodo headed towards the Madelinot, his mind firmly made up to speak to Tania, tell her the truth, but when he walked into the restaurant he realised Robert's machinations had preceded him: no one would look at him and conversations died as he went past, except in the postal workers' corner, where there was open sniggering around Robert, who had a malicious look in his eye and whose nose had turned purplish. When Tania saw him, she acted as if she didn't know him and disappeared into the kitchen.

"Ségolène! Ségolène!" the buffoons wailed languorously at the other end.

Bilodo blanched. Right then he would have given anything to be on the other side of the world. He almost turned on his heel, then remembered he must talk to Tania first, and courageously walked on. Braving the bleatings, puns and other subtle poetic allusions, he went to sit at the counter.

"Ségolène! Take me in your sloop to Guadeloupe!"

Bilodo clenched his fists, not sure how long he'd be able to bear it. Tania came out of the kitchen again with a tray of food. He signalled to her, but she ignored him completely, bringing the postal workers their meals instead. That group wasn't going to let such a wonderful opportunity of teasing her slip by and asked her if she planned to spend her holidays in Guadeloupe this year, if she wasn't too jealous of her rival, if she didn't mind being part of a ménage à trois, and then pointed out that her fiancé, Libido, was waiting for her at the counter and if she hurried, she might end up with another wonderful love poem, just for her this time. Tania finished serving them without saying a word but was obviously fuming. Finally she seemed to think she'd let Bilodo stew long enough, and appeared on the other side of the counter to take his order, so icy she could have sunk a dozen Titanics. What could she get him? Duck – another sitting duck like her? Or a nice little goose, perhaps? A guinea pig to test a new poem on? Deeply apologetic, Bilodo replied she'd got it all wrong, he needed to talk to her in private, but the waitress answered there was no point to that, there was nothing more to say, and she threw a ball of crumpled paper on the counter.

"Here's your poem, Libido!" she spat out.

Clapping broke out in the postal workers' corner and in the rest of the room as well, because Tania definitely had supporters: the entire lunch crowd was following the action with interest. Bilodo pursued the waitress all the way to the kitchen doors, swearing to her in a low voice that it wasn't his fault, the poem hadn't been written for her and should never have been given to her, but Tania, who exuded distrust, wanted to know why he hadn't told her this the day before, instead of letting her make a fool of herself. She then put a stop to Bilodo's mumblings by saying she didn't want to hear about their sick little games any more: let him and Robert find another victim and leave her alone. Another round of applause backed up this rousing command.

Bursting into tears, Tania took refuge in the kitchen, and was replaced in the doorway by Mr Martinez, the establishment's cook, who weighed a good 130 hostile kilos, not counting his kitchen knife. Bilodo saw no option but to retreat, and he dashed out of the place where he was now nothing but an outcast. He wanted to flee as quickly as he could and go and hide at the ends of the earth, but the street swayed under his feet; his legs failed him, and he had to sit down on the steps of the first staircase he came across so as not to collapse.

Five minutes later he was still there, struggling against a feeling of helplessness, doing his best to overcome it, to digest the acidic brew of shame and anger churning in his guts, when the postal workers emerged from the Madelinot, led by Robert. The clerk walked past him, visibly enjoying the sad sight of Bilodo's downfall, and kept going, triumphantly escorted by his minions, who struck up a hymn dedicated to the exotic beauties of the Guadeloupean archipelago. Too weak to protest, Bilodo lowered his eyes and sat staring at the folds of the crumpled tanka he still held in his hand... Then he looked more closely and smoothed it out, noticing suddenly it wasn't the original but another photocopy! Galvanized into action, he called Robert, who was already a hundred metres ahead with his henchmen. The clerk consented to wait for Bilodo as he ran to catch up with him. The time to be subtle being long past, Bilodo demanded Robert give him back his letter. The clerk appeared greatly amused by the request and replied he didn't have his crappy poem any more, he'd simply posted it, then he walked off surrounded by his pack. Bilodo stood stock-still, paralyzed by what he'd just heard: the tanka was on its way.

After all these tribulations, he was back at the starting point.

Enso.

The tanka was travelling inexorably towards Ségolène, and all other concerns had been swept away. Robert's schemes, Tania's heartache, the Post Office, life, death – none of it mattered any more to Bilodo. Had she received the poem? Had she read it? Was she shaken, stunned? Bored, disappointed, scornful? Or quite the opposite: had it touched her, delighted her and was everything perfectly fine? Because Bilodo wanted to favour the second assumption, he found the memory of Tania's initial reaction when she'd read the tanka reassuring: it augured well for Ségolène's response, didn't it? Then the judgement Robert had passed on the poem sprang into his mind and he wasn't sure of anything any more. "Crappy!" the clerk had said. Could he, by some terrible fluke, be right? Bilodo had nightmares about it. In his dreams he saw gigantic lips part and contemptuously utter the word: "Crappy."

And those lips were Ségolène's – those ferociously red lips, those white predatory teeth, that pitiless mouth repeating the murderous word: "Crappy."

And each time it was like a dagger through his heart, because he knew it to be true, his poem was crappy, and she was absolutely right to say it again to punish him for his foolishness. And Ségolène's teeth tore the tanka into a thousand pieces that flitted in all directions, scattering to the furthest reaches of cold nothingness, and on those bits of paper Bilodo could see his own face as though reflected by so many tiny mirrors, his anguish multiplied to infinity...

That's what he dreamt about, and when he woke, he really wasn't sure of anything any more, and was off for another ride on the rollercoaster of fear. He began to ponder if, rather than wait, he should perhaps take preventive action, if he shouldn't write Ségolène and own up to everything, let her know Grandpré was dead and he himself just a pathetic impersonator – at least he'd be easing his conscience – but then he'd change his mind and tell himself to be reasonable again, knowing full well such a confession was impossible, it would have meant giving himself away and ringing the knell of the precious correspondence that was still, and now more than ever, the spice of his life.

Bilodo, as he veered back and forth like a weathercock between hope and resignation, could testify to it: there wasn't anything worse than waiting when you were unsure of the outcome.

— ✉ —

Ségolène's reply finally came. Bilodo rushed out of his cubicle and barricaded himself in the men's toilets. He held his breath, preparing himself to find out what his audacity had cost him, and unfolded the sheet. A five-line poem. She replied with a tanka:

Steamy, sultry night
The moist sheets' soft embrace burns
my thighs and my lips
I search for you, lose my way
I am that open flower

Bilodo blinked, thinking he'd misread it, but no, he hadn't. There was no mistake. Those words were really the words, the lines really those lines, and the poem was that poem.

He had expected a disapproving letter, or perhaps a simple haiku of the kind they used to write to each other, or else, in the most favourable instance, a romantic tanka like his own, but surely not this, this surge of sensuality, this torrid poem. What had come over her? Bilodo felt a stirring in his pelvic region and realised he had an erection, an astonishing physiological occurrence that was all he needed to rattle him completely. Never had a letter from Ségolène provoked such a reaction. Not that it was the first time he had a hard-on in her honour, far from it — it happened all the time when he dreamt about her. But like this, in broad daylight, without the convenient excuse of being unconscious?

It was obviously due to the tanka's unusual content, its palpable eroticism. What he wished he knew was if Ségolène had foreseen the effect her poem might have. Was it accidental or deliberate? How was Bilodo supposed to respond? What could he possibly reply to something like that?

— ✉ —

At night he dreamt about a snake slithering through ferns and crawling furtively among the smooth brown roots of a tree whose trunk was festooned with lianas. Except that the tree wasn't a tree but a body, the naked body of Ségolène asleep with her flute beside her. Quietly, so as not to waken her, the snake crept onto her throat, coiled around her limbs, slid between her breasts, slunk down onto her belly, tasted the air with its bifid tongue, then ventured even further down, towards that dark valley, that bushy triangle between her thighs... Bilodo, enthralled by the serpentine dream, woke up more excited than ever, although this had practically been his normal state since the previous day: his erection persisted, urgent, only vanishing briefly when he managed to put Ségolène's tanka out of his mind. As he reread the stanza, he wondered again if he perceived it correctly, if the sexual coloration he attributed to the poem wasn't a figment of his own depraved imagination, but came to the conclusion it wasn't. The tanka was raunchy, full stop. Whether Ségolène had meant it to be like this or had written it in all innocence, there was only one appropriate way to reply to it:

> You are not just the flower
> You're the whole garden
> Your scents drive me wild
> I enter your corolla
> and I drink in your nectar

As the ocean licks the shore

its surf a salty

kiss – so our lips lightly touch

retreat, draw close again

and lock at last

Chocolate Easter egg

trimmed with a yellow ribbon

The strap of your dress

has slipped down your bare shoulder

which I'd love to nibble on

Tender cannibal
if you nibble me
you will have to eat me whole
or else you will be the one
who is gobbled up by me

I will be the wind
rippling through your hair
stealing its enticing scent
I will slip beneath your skirt
inflaming your skin

My toes are wriggling
coiling and curling
electrified with pleasure
It's because of my fingers
I think too hard about you

— ✉ —

It was a sweet intoxication, a voluptuous fever that made you
live life twice as intensely, a turbulent current you had no desire
to struggle against, a current you could only surrender to, and
besides, that was all Bilodo wanted. His only ambition was to
continue the sensual adventure, the bold detailing of the body, and

experience the ecstasy to the fullest. This pursuit occupied him completely. He hardly ever put his nose outside the door any more and remained indifferent to the loveliness of May, even though he liked that month better than any other. He hadn't gone back to the Madelinot; mortified that Tania could have thought he'd wanted to ridicule her, he daren't show his face there again. Actually, he no longer went to work. The opprobrium he was a victim of at the Depot had become unbearable to him, so he'd asked for and obtained a six-month unpaid leave. Now that his time was his own, he devoted himself entirely to Ségolène.

— ✉ —

Your breasts on the horizon
a dune with satiny slopes
I long to taste their honey
to quench my thirst like
a vampire in love

Lost in the desert
my thirsting mouth crawls along
At last the oasis, where
I dip the tip of my tongue
It is your navel

Your smooth, slender legs catch
the glow of a moonbeam
The sculptor who modelled them
availed himself of
the finest mahogany

Your hands lift me up
bend me, enfold me
fashion me, set me on fire
They do with me what they want
I'm a plaything in your hands

Under the screen of your dress
at the crossing of your thighs
a hidden river
secret Amazon
Let me make my way upstream

The cloth of your skin
sliding over mine
If only I could stitch them
together so they would touch
everywhere at the same time…

— ✉ —

Was the tanka really the best tool when it came to chiselling desire? The form that had served Bilodo so well when it was a matter of putting feelings into words began to weigh him down, seemed too cerebral. Looking for a way to lighten his pen, he decided to go back to the basic simplicity of the haiku, more conducive, he felt, to the gushing forth of artesian urges.

Your breasts – twin mountains
Their proud erectile summits
rise up beneath my fingers

And Ségolène must have appreciated the initiative, since she lost no time in taking the same shortcut:

Robust root throbbing
in the palm of my hand
gorged with burning sap

And so the history of the haiku's birth repeated itself: stripped of superfluous words as though they were clothes dropped on the way to the bedroom, the naked essence of the poetry emerged. But Bilodo wasn't satisfied: he couldn't take the slowness of regular post any more, so he switched to express post. Ségolène followed suit; thus the waiting period was shortened. The exchange sped up, breathing turned into panting, but it still wasn't fast enough for Bilodo, who began to post poems to the Guadeloupean woman without even waiting for her reply and was soon sending her a haiku a day. And Ségolène, too, began sending him haiku after haiku without bothering to wait for his. Almost every morning another letter from her fell on the doormat. The poems flew back and forth, fast and furious, without any chronological continuity now, yet still responding to one another in a peculiar way:

Flower of your flesh
Within its tender petals
lies a hidden pearl

Venture into the
Glowing warmth of me
Lash your body onto mine

I move towards you
Now you let me in
And all your mouths swallow me

You travel in me
you gaze upon my landscape
you swim in my lake

I travel in you
I reach the very centre
of your capital

Seaquake. I explode
deep inside of me
an inner supernova

Fiery tsunami
great surge of lava
I die everlastingly

Carried by the wave
I am nameless now
I am only a colour

Stars – shimmering spread of sails
the solar wind blows
to infinity

You can't have your head in the clouds forever. As gravity eventually caught up with Bilodo, he came back down to earth, still stunned by the slow explosion of the poetic orgasm he'd just experienced. It was true, then, that love gave you wings. Never before had he embraced a woman the way he just did in the heavenly spheres. He'd felt Ségolène so close, sensed her to be all his, totally within him as he'd been totally within her, and knew she, too, had undergone that inner explosion. He was sure she had come at the same time he had. What more could you write after that? What poem could you possibly compose that wouldn't disappoint after passion had been so completely satisfied? Something sweet whispered in the ear of the lover perhaps, before dropping off to sleep?

Searching for an idea, Bilodo put on his kimono, then glanced pensively at the window and saw scattered snowflakes drifting lazily down on rue des Hêtres. Winter already? Had that much time passed? Had summer shot by like a comet without him noticing, indifferent as he'd been to anything outside the boundaries of his inner world? Then, looking more closely, he realised it wasn't snow falling, but pollen raised by the wind, a spray of pollen coming from the trees in the nearby park. You couldn't tell the difference. Winter in the middle of summer. This surreal scene matched Bilodo's mood perfectly and gave him the inspiration for what to write:

Like a duvet on asphalt
a shower of confetti
the first snow softly
languidly settles
on your love-spent night body

— ✉ —

Masquerade of clouds – the moon
slips into nother skin
Tender this moment
on the veranda
when I think only of you

An arid canyon

its rivers and creeks long gone

 where nothing will grow

Such is my desolate soul

between each of your letters

Day in and day out

wherever I am

you are always by my side

Before your poetry, I

didn't know I was alone

The dog is guarding

his sleeping mistress

He's ready to die for her

Allow me, Madam, poor fool

that I am, to be your knight

But you flatter me, dear Sir

I am your humble servant

Still, should it strike your fancy

I will also be

your Dulcinea

Windmills do not frighten me
nor do ferocious giants
All I fear is your
ennui when you see
my sorrowful countenance

On the lycée wall
an ancient clock faithfully
gives the time to the
people in the neighbourhood
My heart beats for you alone

— ✉ —

Glancing by chance at a calendar, Bilodo was amazed to discover that the month of August was already quite far advanced. It would soon be a year since Grandpré had departed this world. The fateful date that had heralded the dramatic change in Bilodo's life was fast approaching, but he felt neither dread nor sadness as the day drew near, because, much more than a death, this anniversary would mark a birth, a rebirth – his own – and the beginning of his tender correspondence with Ségolène. Obviously, the event would only be significant for him: in her eyes it would just be a day like any other, but even so the coming to a close of this first year of bliss seemed worth commemorating, if only in a discreet way:

I was bleak winter

then your poems were my spring

 your love the summer

What has autumn in store for

us with its russets, its gold?

Ségolène's reply, reaching Bilodo a few days later, plunged him into a state of immeasurable horror.

Ségolène had high hopes for the autumn, too...

As a child I dreamt

of Canada's bright autumn I

have bought my ticket and

will arrive the twentieth

Will you have me, then?

The sweet, radiant dream of love was turning into a nightmare. Where did she get such a crazy notion? See the Canadian autumn? What was she driving at?

It was absolutely impossible. Ségolène couldn't show up in Montreal like that, or else it was all over, everything would crumble. How could the delusion continue, since she knew what Grandpré looked like, since there were those blasted photographs they'd exchanged? But how could he tell her not to undertake this insane trip? How was he to say no to her?

She would be coming on the twentieth of September, which gave Bilodo three weeks to find a suitable answer, to fabricate some sort of excuse. Perhaps he could write he'd had to go on a trip himself, that he had to be out of the country for all of September, so unfortunately he wouldn't be able to receive her. But what if she suggested putting off her visit to a later date, to after he got back?

— ✉ —

How could she be so silly? Didn't she realise she would jeopardize everything, she was stupidly endangering the perfect relationship they'd had until then? But of course it wasn't her fault: she couldn't possibly know. Bilodo had to admit he was solely responsible for his misfortune. He should have had the good sense to anticipate what might happen, to guess it would come to this sooner or later. How could he have been so blind?

What to do? Inform her he'd recently undergone cosmetic surgery that had considerably altered his appearance? Or run away? Move immediately out of this apartment she knew the address of and where she'd inevitably turn up as soon as she arrived? Let her deal with the inexplicable mystery of his disappearance on her own? But how would he later be able to bear such a burden of guilt, of cowardice, of dashed hope? How could he forget, how could he survive?

— ✉ —

There was no way out. Bilodo knew he was cornered, as hopelessly caught as an innocent mouse under the cruel steel of the trap. It was the end of the tranquil dream, the bursting of the happy bubble he'd been floating in for so long, and the rupture filled him with helpless anger. He couldn't resign himself to losing her but lacked the courage to face her. All the options were loathsome, all doors were closed. He had reached a terminal dead end.

— ✉ —

It was early the next day when the phone rang. Not caring one way or the other, Bilodo let the answering machine kick in in the living room. Someone was leaving a message. It was a publisher, one of those he'd submitted the manuscript Enso to. The guy briefly explained he liked the collection very much, wanted to publish it, and asked that someone return his call without delay. Unfolding from the fetal position he'd been curled up in, Bilodo got up to go and listen to the message again. Fate sometimes had the oddest twists. This piece of news, which would have delighted him only a day earlier, now merely embittered him. What was the use? What difference could the publication of Grandpré's poems make in the impossibly tangled predicament he was in, except to complicate it even further? Wasn't the game up anyway?

Picking up the manuscript, he opened it at random, as you open a pack of tarot cards in search of a revelation, and came upon this haiku:

To break through the horizon
look behind the set
meet and embrace Death

The poem filled his soul, suddenly took on a new meaning, and Bilodo realised that was it: the only way out, the final solution to all his problems.

He straightened up. He knew what he had to do.

It was perfectly obvious. This was the course he needed to take, but not without first carrying out certain preparations. Bilodo wrote a note to that publisher who just called, giving him permission to publish Enso as he wished. He put the letter on the desk so it would easily be found, then gave Bill a double ration of his favourite yum-yums and said goodbye to the fish, thanking him for his unfailing friendship. He was now ready to go.

The large openwork beam adorning the living room ceiling would do very well. He pushed the little leaf-shaped table directly underneath, then removed the belt from his kimono and tested its strength. Satisfied, he reached into his childhood memories, going back to the carefree days when he belonged to the Cub Scouts, and effortlessly made a slip knot. He was bent on doing things neatly. There was no question of him slitting his wrists or using a gun, two equally disgusting methods. Bilodo wanted to depart this world with dignity, leaving a minimum of traces: hanging was no doubt the least messy way.

He climbed onto the little table, tied the end of the belt to the beam, then tightened the slip knot around his neck. He was ready. It was time to embrace Death. He only had to give a kick with his heel to tip the table and put an end to his suffering. Bilodo took a deep breath, closed his eyes and...

The doorbell pierced the silence.

Bilodo started, not sure what to do. He decided to wait a little while, hoping the intruder would go away, not ring again, but the doorbell sounded a second time. He experienced a peculiar mixture of relief and annoyance. Really! Who dared come and bother him at this crucial moment – he who hadn't had a visit from anyone in months? He removed the slip knot, stepped down from the table, went to the door, and peered through the spy hole. The distorted face that appeared on the other side belonged to Tania.

— ✉ —

Tania. He had almost forgotten about her. If there was one last person to whom Bilodo still owed an explanation, it surely was the young waitress. With a vague feeling of dread, he unlocked the three locks, unlatched the four safety chains, and opened the door. As Tania caught sight of him in the doorway, she seemed even more startled than he was. She stared at him anxiously, asked if he was all right, and blurted out she found him greatly changed. This didn't surprise Bilodo: after so much turmoil, and the serious decision to embrace Death, he must have looked like someone who'd just returned from the grave. With the faintest of reassuring smiles he told her he'd never felt better. The young woman, who appeared unconvinced, apologised for bothering him, and explained in a muddled way she'd got his address through Robert. Bilodo wanted to apologise, too, for what happened at the Madelinot that last time, but she beat him to it, insisted a large part of the blame lay with her: having grilled Robert and got his confession, Tania knew Bilodo wasn't responsible for what had occurred and, besides, she felt it was mostly her own fault, since nothing would have happened if she hadn't indulged in imagining... things, wasn't that true?

She shifted from foot to foot, nervous, visibly embarrassed, looking as though she were waiting for him to confirm what she just said, or contradict it perhaps. Then, when nothing came, she went on to the other purpose of her visit and told him she was going away, she was moving, she was quitting her job at the restaurant to go and live in the suburbs.

Was she hoping for a particular reaction from him? Did his unresponsiveness disappoint her? If so, she didn't let on, but handed him a slip of paper and pointed out it contained her new address in case he... if ever he wanted to... well, anyway... As Bilodo examined the sheet, he noticed she'd taken the trouble to carefully calligraph her new address and phone number Japanese-style, with a brush. The result looked quite lovely, and he complimented her warmly on it. She asked him to get in touch with her if ever it suited him. He promised he definitely would. He really shouldn't hesitate, she added further, forcing a smile. Then there was a brief, awkward silence. They just stood there, on the landing, not saying anything, afraid to look at each other, and this lasted a good ten, interminable, seconds. Finally Tania broke the stasis by telling him she had to go. She said goodbye and stiffly went down the steps.

On the pavement, she turned around to see if he was still there; then, quickening her pace, she hurried off. Bilodo thought he spotted something glistening on her cheek. A tear? When he saw her walk away, a powerful emotion swept over him. It was like a stinging void, like a beautiful thought that aborts just as it is about to take off, vanishing before it has even had a chance to take form. A sharp lump choked Bilodo's throat and he noticed his eyes were blurred with tears. He suddenly felt tempted to call Tania, to hail her before she was too far away, and his hand went up, stretched towards her, and he tried to shout, but no sounds escaped his lips. Once Tania reached the corner, she turned right and slipped out of sight. Bilodo's hand dropped.

On the street, the wind bit its tail, sending newspaper pieces swirling around and around. Bilodo looked up at the sky, saw it was overcast and grey, packed with heavy clouds. There was a storm in the air. He shivered, went back in.

— ✉ —

Bilodo pensively closed the door and studied the sheet of paper with Tania's new address and phone number, no less fascinated by the beautifully calligraphed characters than by the new possibilities they suggested. The letters and figures seemed to float on the surface of the paper, to glow in the dusk. The great change the surprise visit had worked in him baffled Bilodo – that emotion the young woman's tear had stirred up, and that insane hope springing up all of a sudden just from the slip of paper she had left behind. Had he overlooked something terribly important, he wondered? Might there be a solution other than the ones he had considered until then, a better way to get out of the impasse he was in? Could there possibly be life after death or, better still, before?

He walked into the living room and froze, finding himself back in front of the slip knot hanging from the ceiling. He felt his stomach turn. The prospect of dying, which had seemed beneficial only a short while ago, now terrified him, and the thought of the act he had almost committed made him sick. Gripped by a violent wave of nausea, he ran to throw up in the bathroom.

When he finally stood up again, he felt literally drained and had to hold on to the sink so as not to collapse. He needed to freshen up. He ran the cold water, splashed his face numerous times. The wash made him feel a little better. He shook himself off, then cast a pessimistic glance in the mirror, just to see what zombie-like mug would be reflected there.

What he saw frightened him out of his wits. In the mirror loomed the bearded, dishevelled head of Gaston Grandpré.

Bilodo gazed in disbelief at the face that couldn't be there, that shouldn't be there in the mirror instead of his own because it belonged to a dead man. He tried to chase it away by blinking hard, then gave his head a stinging slap, but Grandpré remained stubbornly stuck in the glass, mimicking each of his gestures, watching him with a stupefaction no less than his own. Bilodo came to the obvious conclusion that he had gone mad. Soon after, certain facial details of the mirror's occupant aroused his attention and led him to reconsider this perhaps too-hasty judgement. It wasn't quite Grandpré. Those green eyes were Bilodo's, not the deceased's blue ones, as were those eyebrows – finer, less bushy than Grandpré's – and that slightly flat nose, and the much less fleshy bottom lip... As he slowly recognised himself deep within the other man's face, Bilodo acknowledged he wasn't dreaming, and hadn't slipped into psychosis, and that the guy opposite was really him, though altered in an almost unbelievable way.

Struggling to find a rational explanation, he understood that what he was observing in the glass was the result of a several months' lapse in personal hygiene. He had been so wrapped up in his poetic adventure that he'd completely forgotten to look after himself, neglecting the most basic body care, not even bothering to look at himself in the mirror, so that it had finally come to this: to this visual shock, this decadent image of himself. But – Bilodo wondered – could chance alone account for the extraordinary resemblance to Grandpré? Wasn't it due, rather, to an unconscious wish to identify with his predecessor? Perhaps Bilodo had been so eager to mistake himself for Grandpré he'd ended up looking like him to the point that one could be mistaken for the other. In any case, the illusion was startling: with his several months' growth of beard and his shaggy mane that hadn't seen a comb for just as long, and wrapped in Grandpré's kimono, he bore a striking resemblance to the deceased. No wonder Tania seemed so surprised when she caught sight of him looking like this: for a moment she must have thought she was seeing Grandpré's ghost.

Bilodo decided to tackle the thick beard covering his cheeks right away; he ran the hot water and got out his razor, but stopped in mid-gesture. An idea had just sprung into his mind: since Tania was fooled, even though she'd known the deceased well, and since Bilodo himself had been taken in for a short while, then why couldn't someone who'd only ever seen Grandpré in a photograph be fooled as well?

Transfigured, Bilodo put down his razor. The autumn rendezvous was suddenly becoming possible, wasn't it?

Why not seize this unique chance of welcoming Ségolène to his place? He longed to commune with her through the flesh as much as through words, didn't he? He yearned to love her in another way than in a dream, even though his body would take the place of Grandpré's, to truly love her as she deserved, as they both deserved, and finally start living for real.

Could he ignore such a wonderful opportunity to reverse fate?

Did he even have the right?

So why was he still hesitating? What was keeping him from asking her to come and spend the autumn, the glorious Canadian autumn she had been dreaming about, in his company?

— ✉ —

Fly to the autumn
It's waiting just for you to
display its brilliance

In his euphoria, Bilodo already pictured himself at the airport, welcoming the Guadeloupean woman as she timidly appeared at the arrivals gate, and imagined himself driving along with her through a magnificent, postcard autumn landscape, their hair streaming in the wind. Already he savoured their first kiss, anticipated the fiery first embrace, lost his way in Ségolène's morning hair spilled across the pillow. But for these wonderful visions to become reality, his haiku needed to be posted.

Bilodo had just put a stamp on the envelope when the sky rumbled outside. Thunder. Having threatened all morning, the storm was finally breaking; its first heavy drops crashed against the window glass in the living room. Bilodo refused to let the bad weather stop the poem being sent, so he grabbed an umbrella and went out. While he was still on the landing, a flash of lightning illuminated the street, followed instantly by a loud cracking noise, and suddenly the shower looked like a monsoon. On the other side of the street, through the sheet of rain, he glimpsed a postal van. Post collection time already? It must be, since Robert was there, in the downpour, hurriedly transferring the contents of the box to a sack. Bilodo hesitated. The clerk's presence bothered him. He hadn't spoken to Robert since the spring incidents and had no desire to be subjected to his taunts. Besides, Robert wasn't alone; there was a postman with him, most likely the one substituting for Bilodo in the area, a guy he didn't know, had never even seen, but whom he'd lately grown distrustful of, for he suspected him of trying to open some of Ségolène's letters.

The rain now came down in buckets. Robert, rushing to get out of the storm, closed the postbox again and chucked the sack into the van. He'd be leaving any minute now. Bilodo's wish to post the haiku prevailed over any other consideration: he resigned himself to swallowing his pride and let out a great shout to draw the clerk's attention. Robert turned around, spotted him. Brandishing his letter, Bilodo tore down the stairs and dashed out onto the flooded road. The other guy, the postman, started motioning with his arms, called out something indistinct to him. The blast of a horn pierced the air. Then there was a crash.

The world spun around Bilodo, in slow motion, as in a dream. He whirled around in space, wondering what was happening to him, then there was another crash, and the world became steady again, heavy, and hard beneath his back. The sky flashed and thundered, pelted his eyes with rain. He tried to move, but found he couldn't, and noticed he was in terrible pain. A figure placed itself between the storm and him. A familiar face, Robert's. Then another face appeared, the postman's, familiar too, but for a completely different reason: it was his own. The postman's face was that of the old Bilodo, Bilodo before the metamorphosis, the clean-shaven, clear-eyed Bilodo he had once been.

It was he himself, his former self, looking down at him from up there.

How could he find himself lying on the wet asphalt and be at the same time up there, watching himself? By what magic? Bilodo tried desperately to understand before it was too late, and the answer came to him, it seemed, through an inner voice whispering the words of the opening and closing haiku of Grandpré's collection:

Swirling like water
against rugged rocks
time goes around and around

This was exactly what was happening. The past repeating itself. Time playing a nasty trick on him. As it swirled against the rock – set in the current – that was the moment of Grandpré's death-struggle, time had been caught in a kind of eddy, forming a loop trapping Bilodo.

Had Grandpré sensed this? As he wrote his haiku, had he known it was prophetic?

A life in the shape of a loop. Bilodo had run aground on the shoals of time. This was so unbelievably, so magnificently absurd that in spite of the excruciating pain he could only laugh about it. He laughed, swallowing rainwater, and the more he laughed, the funnier it all seemed to him. Then a lump came into his throat and his laughter ceased. There really wasn't anything amusing about it. In fact, it was tragic: he was dying after all, without any consolation, without the comfort even of knowing his death would be a release, because he only needed to look at the other Bilodo, look at the eager way he eyed the letter between his fingers, to understand that the film wouldn't end here, that his turn would come and the loop would continue, carrying him, too, to his death, and then the one who came after, and the one who followed him as well, and so on forever. It was as cruel as that: Bilodo was condemned to an endlessly recurring death, and nothing could ward off this curse. Except perhaps...

Holding the letter back... preventing it from slipping into the gutter... hanging on to it long enough for the other Bilodo to grab it, maybe read it, and perhaps decide to post it, thus steering his life into a different time stream... and then who knew? The loop might be undone and damnation averted. Mustering whatever strength he had left, he directed it towards the fingers of his right hand, which tightened on the letter. He closed his eyes the better to focus his willpower, and an unusual image appeared on the screen of his closed eyelids: a red circle or, rather, a revolving wheel of fire.

Still the cursed loop. The serpent bit its tail. Time cannibalized itself.

Suddenly, in Bilodo's mind, the memory resurfaced of those obscure syllables, those final words Grandpré had murmured just before he expired: "in-sole", he thought he heard. He hadn't understood at the time what it was about, but now he knew with dazzling certainty.

"Enso." he moaned as the last breath of life abandoned him.